The Jade Dragon

The Jade Dragon

CAROLYN MARSDEN
AND VIRGINIA SHIN-MUI LOH

CANDLEWICK PRESS
CAMBRIDGE, MASSACHUSETTS

We would like to acknowledge the San Diego Chinese Historical Society and Museum for help with the calligraphy and translation; Pao-in "Bella" Liu for her translation; Gretchen Woelfle for encouragement in the early stages; and our editors, Deborah Wayshak and Amy Ehrlich, for their continued support and guidance. We would also like to thank friends, family, and our critique group, the Snail Society.

First edition 2006

While every effort has been made to obtain permission to reprint copyright material, there may be cases where we have been unable to trace a copyright holder. The publisher will be happy to correct any omission in future printings.

Library of Congress Cataloging-in-Publication Data
Marsden, Carolyn.
The jade dragon / Carolyn Marsden and Virginia Shin-Mui Loh. —1st ed.
p.   cm.
Summary: A Chinese-American girl torn between her family's
traditional values and the more modern ones in her second grade
classroom learns that friendship cannot be bought.
ISBN-13: 978-0-7636-3012-6
ISBN-10: 0-7636-3012-8
[1. Chinese Americans—Fiction. 2. Friendship—Fiction. 3. Identity—Fiction.]
I. Loh, Virginia Shin-Mui. II. Title.
PZ7.M35135Jad 2006
[E] —dc22   2006042572

2 4 6 8 10 9 7 5 3 1

Printed in the United States of America

This book was typeset in Leawood Book.

Candlewick Press
2067 Massachusetts Avenue
Cambridge, Massachusetts 02140

visit us at www.candlewick.com

For my dear friend Julie M. Willson
C. M.

To Tamara, Phyllis, and Bill
V. S. L.

Chapter One

"We go together. . . . Chang-chang changity-chang shoo-bop. That's the way it should be. . . ." was playing from Robin's boom box.

Robin, her long orange braid swinging in the cold air, and a girl Ginny had never seen before were holding hands and dancing to the song.

The new girl had straight black hair that shone in the sun, just like Ginny's. She had bangs cut straight across, just like Ginny's.

Another Chinese girl. The only other Chinese girl in the whole second grade. Ginny's heart did a little dance. She smiled and took her hands out of her pockets. Maybe this Chinese girl would be her best friend.

She got invited to birthday parties and played with kids at recess. Sometimes a girl would even invite her over. But she'd never had a *best friend,* someone to share special secrets with. Even though Ginny now spoke good English—without an accent—none of the white girls wanted to be her best friend.

Maybe this Chinese girl would.

Ginny moved slightly in time to Robin's music. She wished she were closer to the girl. Robin already had lots of friends. She didn't need another.

When the bell rang, all the kids on the playground ran into line. Ginny followed the girl as she rushed to the front.

Robin lined up for the other second grade, waving and smiling at the Chinese girl.

Even though Ginny ran fast in her rubber boots, she ended up in the back.

She leaned so far out of the line to look at the new girl that Mrs. Vincent said, "Ginny Liao, stand up straight, please."

Ginny stood tall, with her arms at her sides.

Inside the classroom hung snowflake mobiles. All the words the class could spell covered one wall, and the date was written neatly on the chalkboard: December 12, 1983.

Mrs. Vincent said, "Stephanie, please sit here, right in front of Ginny." She tapped her finger on an empty desk.

Ginny expected the girl to turn around and smile at her. Surely, she would be looking for a Chinese friend. But Stephanie kept her back to Ginny.

Why was she acting so unfriendly?

"Boys and girls, this is Stephanie Bronelle, our new student," Mrs. Vincent announced.

Bronelle? Why did a Chinese girl have an American last name?

All morning, Stephanie bent over her work sheets of addition problems with the smiling snowmen around the borders.

After doing each problem on her own sheet, Ginny looked up at Stephanie's hair, the light shining on it every time she moved her head.

Maybe at recess this girl would talk to her.

But on the playground, Stephanie ran ahead, dashing across the blacktop in her winter boots, her bright green scarf sailing out behind her.

Ginny stood against the monkey bars, the cold metal pressing into her back through her puffy jacket.

Even though she was brand new, Stephanie took Robin's hand and they both began to chase Ricky. As they went back and forth across the playground, around the swings, and under the slide, Ginny felt as though she were running after Ricky herself, her heart beating a little faster whenever the girls got close.

Finally, they chased him into a corner of the playground and grabbed him. Ginny's hands closed as though she, too, held Ricky's arm.

"Come on, Ricky, be the baby. Robin and I are playing house and we need you to be the little baby," Stephanie said loudly.

Ricky pulled loose.

Robin linked her arm through Stephanie's arm. "You and me. We go together, don't we?"

Stephanie giggled.

Me too, me too, a little voice called out inside Ginny. She wanted to go together too.

Stephanie and Robin ran to the monkey bars, where Ginny was standing.

Ginny stared at Stephanie's narrow eyes, at her round face like a beautiful full moon.

"I can't wait for Santa to come to my house!"

Stephanie said, grabbing onto a bar and swinging back and forth.

Lately, everyone was talking about Santa. Ginny just listened.

"I want a *Star Wars* light saber." Ricky held out his arm and pretended to slash the air.

"I asked for a Princess Leia doll," said Robin.

Suddenly, Stephanie turned to Ginny. "Hey, what do you want Santa to bring you?"

"Santa?" Ginny looked around, over her shoulder.

"I'm talking to you. Don't you know about Santa?"

"Of course I know who Santa is. Everybody knows." Santa was for white kids. He'd never come to her house.

As though he was reading Ginny's thoughts, Ricky said, "Santa doesn't go to China."

Stephanie stared straight at him and said, "Santa does too go there. The elves used to work at the North Pole, but now they work in China. Haven't you seen 'Made in China' on your toys?"

Ginny couldn't help smiling.

Stephanie spoke to Ginny again. "Well, what do you want Santa to bring you?"

They all stared at her, waiting for an answer.

Santa had never brought her anything. Why should he now? "A doll," she finally said.

"That's all?" Stephanie asked.

"A light saber."

The kids giggled.

"What else?" Stephanie asked.

I want to go together with you, Ginny thought.

"Hey, I know," said Stephanie, "let's write letters to Santa!" She rummaged through her backpack and pulled out a chunky blue pencil and a pad of paper. "If we write him, he'll bring us whatever we want."

Ginny had never thought about writing to Santa. Maybe that was the problem. Santa didn't know about her. Other kids wrote to Santa and he went to their houses.

Robin got out a pencil with a tiny troll doll perched on the eraser end.

Stephanie and Robin knelt down on the playground and began to write. Stephanie clamped her tongue between her front teeth and Robin leaned so close that her orange braid brushed the paper.

"I hate writing letters," said Ricky, walking away.

Stephanie glanced up at Ginny. "Don't you want anything? Here." She tossed a piece of paper in Ginny's direction.

Ginny knelt down, took off her mittens and laid them next to the paper.

Mrs. Vincent had dolls in the second grade classroom that the girls played with during free time. Ginny loved to dress the dolls in beautiful clothes, pretending that they were going to fancy parties. She could ask Santa for a doll.

Then, she had another thought. Could Santa make this new girl, this Stephanie Bronelle, her best friend?

Ginny began to write, her letters wobbly as her pencil moved over the nubby asphalt of the playground.

"Now we do like this," said Stephanie sitting back on her heels. She folded her paper in half, then pulled out a sheet of stickers—rows of Santa Clauses holding their fat bellies. "These are special Santa stamps. Close your paper up with these and you don't need an envelope."

Ginny took the sheet from Stephanie, peeled off a sticker, and sealed her wishes tightly. On the front, she wrote: *North Pole.*

Chapter Two

"What is this?" MaMá took the sealed paper from Ginny's book bag. *"North Pole?"*

"We wrote letters to Santa Claus today."

"How can you mail this? No such place is this North Pole." MaMá looked more closely. "You put on a sticker. The post office needs a stamp."

"Santa doesn't need stamps because he has a special mailman."

MaMá just shook her head and started opening

the letter, using her long red fingernail to un-seal it.

"MaMá! You can't open Santa's letter!"

But she did. She spread the paper neatly on the dining-room table, the light shining down on it.

December 1983

Dear Mr. Santa Claws,

I have bin good this year. Exep for the late libary book. But I gave it back and my grades are realy, realy good.

For Crismas, please give me a best friend. Theres a girl in my class I want to be best friends with. She is Chinez like me. Maybe you could make her like me.

I also want a doll.

Your friend,
Ginny

"Hmm. How come you do not put your Chinese name? *Xin Mei* is a very good name. Your *babá* and I had to think very hard about your name."

Ginny sighed. MaMá always asked that. "MaMá, in American school, people just use their American names."

"That's silly." MaMá looked at the letter again. "Why did you write this letter, Ah Mei?" MaMá called her by her nickname. It meant *Beautiful Little Heart.*

"If you write to Santa, he'll give you what you want for Christmas."

MaMá shrugged. "I hear this Santa walks on the roofs."

"Yes, he comes down the chimney, remember?" Ginny wasn't sure that MaMá knew the word, so she pointed toward the chimney.

MaMá turned to stare at the fireplace. "Well, I

will have BaBá check the roof to make sure that it is strong."

MaMá squinted at the letter again. "Who is this girl? She is Chinese?"

"Yes, MaMá. Stephanie's the new girl in my class. I think she lives close by."

"Oh, I saw a big moving truck. It is good that she is Chinese. You will make friends with her easy since you have things in common." She picked up her Chinese newspaper and started reading it.

Suddenly, Ginny had an idea that would get MaMá more interested in Santa.

This idea would also make Santa pay more attention to her letter. He received lots of letters that looked the same. What if Ginny's letter were written in MaMá's beautiful Chinese characters that went up and down like in her newspaper? Santa would have to take special notice, wouldn't he?

"I need your help, MaMá. Could you write this letter in Chinese for me?"

"You want me to write in Chinese for you? Ah Mei, your *mamá* is very happy." She put down her newspaper.

MaMá collected her calligraphy supplies from the cabinet.

Ginny leaned close as MaMá laid out the special rice paper that crinkled and let the light shine through. She watched carefully as MaMá poured the thick black ink onto the ink stone.

As MaMá mixed the ink and the water with a tiny silver spoon, she hummed a Chinese song about chasing the moon, and Ginny hummed too.

MaMá put all four of her fingers on top of the brush. Her thumb held the bamboo at a right angle to the table. "Ah Mei, I do not know if there is a Chinese word for your Santa person. But this is the Chinese character for *claws,* like tiger claws. A tiger is a very powerful animal, like your *babá.*"

"That is good, MaMá." *Mr. Claws* would be enough.

MaMá swished the brush over the newspaper, making a scratchy noise.

Ginny loved the way the black ink seeped into the paper. The beautiful strokes of ink looked more like painting than writing.

"We will put your Chinese name on it," MaMá said, writing the characters for *Liao Xin Mei*.

"It looks really good, MaMá."

MaMá and Ginny blew on the rice paper to make the ink dry faster. MaMá smiled, then handed over the letter.

Santa would love it.

Ginny took a big black marker and wrote *Ginny* right next to the pretty Chinese characters.

"Ah Mei!" MaMá exclaimed. "Now you have ruined the whole thing!"

"But what if Santa doesn't read Chinese? At least he will know who the letter is from."

MaMá shook her head and sighed. She rinsed the black ink from the brush. The blackness mixed with the water, making a gray puddle in the white sink. She rolled up the rice paper and put it in its cardboard tube.

Ginny took a dry paper towel and pressed the hairs of the brush dry. She placed the ink stick, the mixing stone, and the brush into the case, matching the tools to the shapes imprinted in the red velvet. Before she closed the lid, she ran her fingertip over the velvet—red, just like Santa's suit.

When everything was cleaned up and the letter was dry, MaMá asked, "Now what will you do with your letter?"

"Mail it." Ginny put on her coat, then skipped to the mailbox on the corner, humming the tune to MaMá's Chinese song.

Chapter Three

MaMá scooped rice from the bucket in the pantry and poured it into the silver rice cooker. She ran water into the cooker and turned it on.

"Here, Ah Mei, you chop these spring onions." She gave her a bundle of green onions and a sharp knife.

MaMá began to clean shrimp, pulling the black veins loose.

After Ginny had cut the onions into tiny pieces, MaMá handed Ginny a bowl with the blue-gray shrimp she'd split open. "Wash the shrimp."

While MaMá broke up dried chilies for the red shrimp marinade, Ginny washed each slippery shrimp under running water. "Is Daddy coming home tonight?" she asked.

BaBá liked it when Ginny called him Daddy.

MaMá always made shrimp for Daddy, especially if he'd been gone. "Yes. BaBá called. He will be home, but he has to work late again."

"Daddy always has to work late." Ginny dropped a shrimp and picked it up from the sink.

"Ah Mei, you know that he has to work a lot, especially when he is getting ready to travel."

"Where's he going this time?"

"To California."

"What about Christmas?"

"No big deal. That is an American holiday." MaMá slid Ginny's onions onto an empty plate. "I hope he gets back home before snow comes. This is a bad time for air traveling."

But Daddy just had to be home for Christmas! The onions suddenly made Ginny's eyes water. She washed her hands with soap to get the smell off her fingers.

"Ah Mei. Do not worry so much." MaMá nudged Ginny with her elbow. "He will be back for the Christmas party."

"Christmas party?"

"We will have the big party for BaBá's work people."

"At our house?"

"Yes, Ah Mei."

Daddy worked in Washington, D.C., in a building called the Pentagon. Because he spoke many languages, the government sent him to other countries.

At Daddy's office, Ginny liked to see people's

uniforms decorated with shiny medals, ribbons, and stripes.

"May I invite that Chinese girl to the party?"

"The new girl?" MaMá stirred the marinade and added a cupful of black beans. "Is she your friend now?"

"She's not my friend yet."

"Did you talk to her today?"

"No. It was only her second day. I didn't want to bother her." Ginny's voice dropped.

It had been Ginny's turn to choose something from Mrs. Vincent's box of playground equipment.

She'd lifted the bouncy rubber ball into the crook of her arm. She'd held the jump rope in her other hand.

Which one would Stephanie want to play with? Which one would get Stephanie to talk to her? Boys liked balls; girls liked jump ropes. Ginny had let the ball tumble back into the box.

But during recess, Stephanie didn't look at her

standing with the jump rope. She played the chasing game with Robin and Ricky again.

Ginny had just watched, the jump rope in her hand.

"Was the new girl busy with her schoolwork?" MaMá asked.

"No, she has other friends."

"But these friends are not Chinese?"

"No, MaMá. Stephanie likes white kids."

"Hmph."

While MaMá cooked, her big chopsticks dancing in the wok, Ginny played a detective game with MaMá's Chinese newspaper. She couldn't read the characters, so she pretended to break the secret code.

The Chinese characters looked like stick pictures to Ginny. Some looked like puppy dogs wagging their tails. Some formed houses. Others looked like rib bones.

"Look, MaMá." Ginny, playing the game,

pointed to a headline. "This says: 'A rabbit found a hole under a bush.'"

MaMá laughed and spoke to herself in Chinese.

The door burst open, and there was Daddy. "Surprise!"

"Daddy!" Ginny ran to him and pressed her face against his chest.

"Mmm. You smell like, like . . ."

"Shrimp? Onion?" she mumbled into his jacket.

"That's it. A little fishy. A little oniony."

He lifted her up and kissed her cheek, then leaned over and kissed MaMá's cheek.

"Sit down," MaMá said. "Dinner is ready."

"Just in time, right, Ah Mei?" Daddy winked at her.

MaMá hovered over Ginny's plate and spooned out rice, then shrimp—now cooked and pink—and finally, the thick red sauce with black beans.

"Ah Mei has a new Chinese girl in her class," MaMá said.

"What's her name, Ah Mei?" Daddy asked.

"Stephanie," Ginny answered.

"Her family lives close," MaMá said. "But I have not seen them yet."

"I wonder if they'll send her to Chinese School over at Annandale High School. Maybe she and Ginny could go together."

"It is about time Ah Mei went," said MaMá.

"How about it, Ah Mei?" Daddy asked.

Ginny nodded, her mouth full of shrimp. She wanted to go to Chinese School. MaMá had said they taught calligraphy there. And if Stephanie went too, that would be perfect.

"After the holidays, we'll look into it," said Daddy.

Later that night, Ginny went downstairs to get a glass of water. She heard MaMá and Daddy in the living room, speaking Chinese with English words sprinkled in.

Ginny stood in the kitchen, sipping the water. She could understand only a word here and there of the Chinese. MaMá and Daddy were probably talking about his work or his trip to California.

Then she heard the name *Miss Fortmann.* Ginny held the glass with both hands. Miss Fortmann had been her kindergarten teacher. Miss Fortmann with the long yellow braid and flowered skirts. Were MaMá and Daddy talking again about how Ginny had spoken only Chinese in kindergarten? Were they talking about the past again?

Ginny had been born a year after MaMá and Daddy had come to America. Daddy loved to talk about how he'd named his new baby Virginia, after the state they lived in.

But even though they loved America and their new state, MaMá and Daddy hadn't spoken English to Ginny. Until she'd gone to kindergarten, Ginny had known only Chinese.

Ginny heard the words *Miss Fortmann* again. She set the glass in the sink. Her bare feet were cold, but she listened harder, trying to understand.

Daddy said the English words *Chinese School.* Were they talking about sending her? She'd gone to American school to forget Chinese, and now they wanted her to go to Chinese School to remember it.

When she was in kindergarten, she'd overheard another conversation in Chinese between MaMá and Daddy. But back then, she'd understood every word.

"That Miss Fortmann says that Ah Mei has to learn English. She says no more Chinese. Not at home. Not anywhere," MaMá had said.

"Ginny needs to speak English to be successful here in America. You know that," Daddy had said soothingly.

"That is fine for you to say, Kai. You know English. For me, English is very difficult."

"Maybe if you speak to Ah Mei in English, your own will get better."

"Ha! Two of us learning from each other then? Two who know nothing? Liao Kai, you cannot tell me that it is best that my daughter cannot speak to me. That I cannot speak to her. That we cannot speak our own language. What is that teacher saying?"

"We are in America now, Suling. We must do what the American teacher says."

There had been a long pause, then MaMá's voice, quiet now: "I will do it, Kai. But it does not make me happy."

From that day on, Ginny had to get rid of all the Chinese words in her head, in her mouth, and in her heart. She had to say English words that felt like stale buns in her mouth. The words made no more sense than the barking of dogs or the chirping of birds.

She had to listen to those nonsense English words said even by her own *mamá* and *babá*.

For a long time, Ginny had had no words at all, but now she was used to English and hardly understood the language she grew up speaking.

Chapter Four

MaMá pulled the Lincoln Town Car close to the curb a block from school. She hated getting into the school traffic. "Why does everyone rush around so much? People are always in a hurry in America."

In the distance, Ginny saw Stephanie going up the steps into the school, her pink earmuffs clamped over her black hair.

"There she is, MaMá!"

"Good. You need a Chinese friend."

Ginny got out of the car and walked quickly. Maybe Stephanie would notice her.

Together, they went through the big red doors, then walked down the hallway, their winter boots clicking along together as if they were marking the beat to the same song. The hallway smelled of erasers and pencil lead, mixed with a sugary sweetness from the cafeteria breakfast.

They were two Chinese girls walking side by side down the hall.

Stephanie held the classroom door open while Ginny went inside. Still without saying anything, they bent over, side by side, and put their jackets, mittens, and scarves in their cubbies.

At lunch, Ginny let two girls and a boy ahead of her in line so that when she sat down at the table, she would be right across from Stephanie.

Stephanie had a Princess Leia lunch box. The princess's hair was coiled over her ears, and she smiled at Luke Skywalker in the distance.

Ginny's lunch was in a brown bag. She pulled out a Tupperware container of rice with *chau-su,* bright red roasted pork. "Would you like to try some?" she asked Stephanie. Everyone loved MaMá's cooking.

Stephanie looked at the plastic container and wrinkled her nose. Her narrow eyes grew narrower. "I don't really eat Chinese food."

Not eat Chinese food? How could that be?

"But aren't you Chinese?"

Stephanie shrugged.

Ginny held up the orange that MaMá had cut to look like a blooming flower. "How about this?"

"It's pretty. Okay, I'll try it." Stephanie bit into the orange and made a face. "It's *salty*! But I kinda like it." She ate the rest and licked the salt from her fingers.

Ginny took a bite of pork.

Stephanie had eaten the orange, but wouldn't

try the *chau-su*. Why didn't she want to eat Chinese food?

After lunch, Mrs. Vincent said, "We're going to start math relays today, boys and girls. I'll assign teams for this week."

Ginny kept her fingers crossed under her desk. *Please listen, Santa, oh please . . .*

Mrs. Vincent divided the class into pairs, reading out the names from her roll sheet: "Amber and John, Steven and Brent . . ."

Finally, she read: "Ginny and Stephanie."

Yes! Oh, yes! Santa must have already gotten her letter!

Ginny reached out and tapped Stephanie on the shoulder.

Stephanie turned around and smiled a little.

Ginny smiled back.

"And now, boys and girls, please line up with

your partners." They formed two lines with five pairs in each. Mrs. Vincent moved the desks aside and got out her flash cards.

As Mrs. Vincent held up addition problems— 51 + 12, 29 + 64—the two pairs of partners at the front of their lines rushed to the chalkboard to figure out the answers. The pair that got the answer first went to the back of their line; the other pair sat down.

Finally, it was Ginny and Stephanie's turn to compete; they were going against Louis and Christine.

Mrs. Vincent's flash card read: 52 + 79.

All four ran to the front of the room and grabbed pieces of chalk.

"One hundred thirty-one," Ginny and Stephanie said at the same time.

They had beaten Louis and Christine.

Stephanie held out her palm.

Ginny slapped it. "High five," she said.

They waited their next turn at the back of their line.

Ginny stood on one foot, then the other. She and Stephanie had to win; they just had to. Her tummy rumbled.

When Mrs. Vincent called their names again, she held up 63 + 18. Again, they rushed to the chalkboard, wrote fast, and got the right answer first.

Finally, there was only one other pair left: Ricky and Linda.

When Mrs. Vincent showed the problem, the four ran, wrote, and shouted out the answer at the same time.

It seemed like a tie, but Mrs. Vincent said, "I think I heard Ginny's voice just a second before the others."

Ginny and Stephanie jumped up and down and slapped each other with many high fives. They'd done it! They'd won!

Mrs. Vincent brought them to the front of the

room. She put her arms around their shoulders. "These two make a good team," she said.

At lunch recess, Stephanie tied one end of the jump rope to the monkey bars and handed the other end to Ginny. Their mittens touched just for an instant.

Ginny turned the rope while Stephanie jumped. She turned the rope for Robin and other girls too. She turned the rope carefully, lifting her arm in a big, even circle so that no one would miss because of her.

"Now you, Ginny," Stephanie said at last.

Robin sang the alphabet song as Ginny jumped.

Each time she went up, she felt as though she would never come down.

* * *

Dear Ginny,

Please come over to my house tomorrow
after school to play.

Sincerely, Stephanie

Ginny stared at the note. Stephanie's printing was so nice—the lines straight, the circles round. It looked different from her usual writing. She must have worked on the note for a long time.

Ginny folded the paper into a neat rectangle and tucked it into the pocket of her blouse, close to her heart.

Stephanie glanced back, and Ginny gave her a little wave. A little wave that meant *Yes, oh yes.* She lifted the lid of her desk just enough to slide her hand inside. She slipped out a piece of paper and a pencil and wrote *Yes!!!*

* * *

"MaMá," Ginny said as she got in the car and slammed the door, "I have a best friend." She patted the note in her pocket, making sure it was still there. "She wants me to visit her house."

"Who?"

"The Chinese girl I told you about." MaMá *couldn't* say no.

MaMá slowed the car way down. "You must give me this girl's phone number. I will talk to her mother, and we will see. At her house, remember to take off your shoes."

Instead of thinking of shoes, Ginny imagined fixing Stephanie's hair—braiding it, making pigtails, pinning it back with barrettes. Then Stephanie could fix Ginny's hair exactly the same. They'd look in the mirror together.

At dinner, Ginny ate MaMá's noodles with oyster sauce without tasting them. On TV, she'd watched best friends jumping on the bed and throwing pillows at each other, shrieking with laughter.

At bedtime, Ginny pictured writing Stephanie's phone number in a little book. Stephanie would write hers in a little book too. She fell asleep humming the tune to "We Go Together."

Chapter Five

After school, Stephanie ran down the school steps ahead of Ginny. "Mommy," she cried, throwing her arms around a white lady. The lady wore navy blue heels that matched her suit.

Ginny stared. How could this be Stephanie's mom? This lady had round blue eyes and light brown hair that ended in a big curl that just touched her shoulders.

The lady hugged Stephanie and kissed her on the cheek. Then, to Ginny's surprise, she reached down and gave *her* a hug too. No one ever hugged her except for Mrs. Vincent and Daddy.

"You must be Ginny," she said, still holding on to her.

Ginny nodded, moving her head up and down against the dark blue material of the lady's suit.

"I'm Stephanie's mother. My name is Mrs. Bronelle, but you may call me Tamara," she said.

Ginny looked down at the sidewalk. MaMá wouldn't like her to call Stephanie's mom by her first name. She shook her head slightly.

"How about Mrs. B., then?" Mrs. Bronelle said.

Ginny nodded. That would be okay.

But how could this white lady be Stephanie's mom?

"How lovely for you to have a Chinese friend, Stephanie," Mrs. B. said.

Oh yes. Ginny thought. *For me too. And for MaMá.* Ginny felt the tap-tap of her happy heart.

"Your mother called and left a message. I'm

looking forward to talking to her when she comes to pick you up this afternoon."

The tappity dance stopped for a moment. So MaMá didn't know yet that Stephanie's mom was white. She would be so surprised. But would it be a good surprise?

"How nice to have a Chinese friend, sweet-heart," Mrs. B. said to Stephanie again.

But Stephanie was waving good-bye to Ricky, who was running up and down the school steps.

Mrs. B. asked Stephanie, "What did you do in school today?"

"Nothing," Stephanie answered.

That wasn't true. Mrs. Vincent had read an-other chapter of *The Snow Queen,* and they had written stories about the North Pole. At the end of the day, everyone had sat in a circle to sing "Frosty the Snowman."

Mrs. B. took Stephanie's hand, and then she took Ginny's hand. She gave it a big squeeze.

They walked to the car holding hands. Mrs. B.'s heels clicked on the sidewalk as she walked.

Mrs. B.'s white car had a little metal star on the hood. The license plate said MY BENZ.

Ginny climbed into the dark blue inside that matched Mrs. B.'s blue suit and heels. She moved over so that Stephanie could get in the back-seat beside her. Finally, it was happening—she was going to her best friend's house. Ginny imagined the two of them looking out the window together, pointing and laughing at things they passed.

Instead, Stephanie got in the front.

Ginny held the strap of her seat belt but didn't fasten it. Did Stephanie mean for her to get in front with her? It didn't seem like it. Stephanie didn't make room for Ginny by moving close to her mom. She expected Ginny to stay in the back.

Why didn't Stephanie want to sit with her?

"Do your parents come from China, Ginny?"

Mrs. B. asked, looking at Ginny in the rearview mirror.

"Yes, Mrs. B."

"Stephanie comes from China too. She came to us when she was just a little baby."

What did Mrs. B. mean by that? Had Stephanie been brought to them by a stork— the bird that carried babies in slings to their new parents—like in one of Mrs. Vincent's stories?

"How nice, Mrs. B.," Ginny said.

Stephanie scooted closer to the window and pressed her forehead against the glass.

There were no shoes lined up by the door at Stephanie's house. Mrs. B. clicked right into the house in her heels. Stephanie marched in with her winter boots. Ginny paused, thinking of what MaMá had said about shoes, then decided to keep her boots on.

Moving boxes were piled high along the wall

of the kitchen, and the cupboard doors were wide open. On one wall hung a big map of China with a star on it.

"Excuse the mess, Ginny. We just moved in." Mrs. B. pointed to the star on the map. "That's where Stephanie was born."

Stephanie rolled her eyes.

Mrs. B. kicked her heels into the corner of the kitchen—MaMá would have screwed up her face if she'd seen that—and threw her suit jacket onto a chair.

Ginny lifted a container of steamed pork buns out of her book bag. "My mom made these for you." The buns smelled delicious—like doughy bread with a hint of sweet meat inside.

Mrs. B. leaned over to glance at them. "These are Chinese buns, Stephanie. They're like Chinese hamburgers." She reached for one and took a bite. "Mmm. Want to try one, honey?"

"No, thanks. I'll have a sandwich."

"How about you, Ginny? A sandwich or one of these buns?"

Ginny loved steamed buns. But she never passed up a chance to eat American food. "A sandwich, please."

"Well, I'm going to have one of these buns. Please thank your mother." From the refrigerator, Mrs. B. got out a loaf of bread. She peeled plastic off the slices of cheese. "One day, Stephanie, I want to take you back to China."

"I don't want to go to China. I want to go to Australia."

Stephanie began to flip through a magazine. She stopped and held up a page. It was an ad for shampoo. The girl's hair was like a blond waterfall. "This is the kind of hair I'm going to have when I grow up."

Mrs. B. laughed, but Ginny noticed that she also pinched her eyebrows together in a little frown. "You and Ginny have such beautiful hair. Why would you want to ruin it?"

"I hate how black it is," said Stephanie.

Ginny touched her own black hair. Should she hate it?

Mrs. B. set the plate in front of Ginny. There was a pile of potato chips by the sandwich.

Ginny picked up her sandwich and bit into it. The precious white bread stuck to the roof of her mouth.

"Kool-Aid?" Mrs. B. offered a pitcher of bright purple sugar water.

Ginny nodded. When she got home, she would have to hide her purple tongue from MaMá.

When they finished the sandwiches, Stephanie kept studying the magazine.

Ginny looked down at her hands and waited.

"I am so happy that you came over today. I've been asking Stephanie to invite you over ever since I saw you," Mrs. B. said, wiping her hands on a dish towel.

"Mom!" Stephanie rolled her eyes.

"What?" Mrs. B. dropped the towel onto the counter. "It's important for you to have Chinese friends."

Stephanie rolled her eyes again.

Ginny pinched a bread crumb that lay on the edge of her empty plate. So it had been Mrs. B.'s idea to have her come over. She remembered the note. Suddenly, she knew that Mrs. B. had written it, not Stephanie. Even after she and Stephanie had won the math relays, it wasn't Stephanie who'd invited her to play. Stephanie was not her best friend after all.

Ginny put the bread crumb in her mouth. She wished that MaMá would come right now and take her home.

As Mrs. B. picked up the plates, she said, "Why don't you show Ginny your room, sweetheart?

I'm sure she doesn't want to watch you read a magazine."

On the wall along the stairs were photos of Mrs. B. and Stephanie and also a white man who had to be Mr. B. His hair covered only the sides of his head, but it was a nice light color with silver streaks. His big smile showed a lot of teeth.

Stephanie didn't look like her father.

The first thing Ginny saw in Stephanie's room was the canopy bed with white see-through curtains. Little tassels hung from the edges of the curtains, and fat lacy pillows were piled at the head of the bed.

Ginny peeked into the closet at the row of pretty dresses and blouses. She saw a pink dress wrapped in clear plastic.

"That's my holiday dress," Stephanie said.

"It's so pretty," said Ginny. For a moment, she laid her hand on the plastic cover, feeling the slick pink nylon underneath.

In Stephanie's room, a dollhouse with real miniature furniture sat on the window ledge. Below that rested a basket of plastic ponies—turquoise, pale pink, lemon yellow, purple—with hair you could comb. A trunk overflowed with Barbies, troll dolls, Cabbage Patch dolls with their funny, smashed faces, cloth Holly Hobbie dolls, and Strawberry Shortcake dolls wearing poofy hats and dresses with poofy sleeves.

Every one of the dolls had blond hair. None had brown or black. Ginny thought of what Stephanie had said about her own black hair.

Ginny stood still, looking from one doll to the next. It was like being in a toy store.

"May I hold one?" she asked Stephanie.

"Sure."

Ginny picked up a doll dressed in green shorts and a red top. She breathed in the sharp plastic smell.

Stephanie turned on a TV on a shelf above

her bed. She lay back on the pillow and began to watch.

Ginny's eyes grew wide. "*Mork and Mindy*! MaMá doesn't let me watch that. She says there's no such thing as aliens."

"Of course there are. Here," Stephanie patted a place beside her on the bed.

Ginny sat very straight against the pillows, watching a funny-talking man chase a woman around a living room, grabbing for her ear.

When the show ended, Stephanie flipped through the channels and sighed. "Nothing good's on. Do you want to color?"

Ginny nodded. She would *love* to color.

Stephanie got a coloring book from the drawer and a box of sixty-four crayons. The crayons were all the colors that Ginny had ever imagined, including silver and gold.

"Why don't you do this one?" Stephanie opened the page to a picture of a unicorn. "Be careful not to color messy, though. All my pictures are neat." She flipped back to show ponies and dolls, all filled in with even strokes, no mistakes outside the lines.

Ginny set the doll on her lap and began to color, holding the crayon tight.

Stephanie didn't color in a coloring book. She took a blank piece of paper and drew a princess.

As Ginny used gray on the unicorn's horn, Stephanie made the princess's hair longer and longer, blonder and blonder, swirling down past her feet.

Ginny finished the unicorn and was just starting on the sky behind, when the doorbell rang. Ginny recognized MaMá's loud voice, then heard Mrs. B.'s voice. They were talking together in the entranceway below.

Ginny laid the doll and the coloring book on the bed, letting go of them slowly. "My mom's here," she said to Stephanie.

"Okay," Stephanie said, not taking her eyes off her drawing.

Ginny went down the stairs. With each step, she felt herself sink away from Stephanie and her room of toys. Would she ever climb these stairs again?

MaMá looked up at Ginny, then down at her feet in the winter boots. She frowned.

Then Ginny noticed her studying the family photos on the wall. Surely, MaMá noticed that Stephanie looked totally different from both her parents. What was she thinking?

"Well, good-bye," MaMá said, taking Ginny's hand. "Thank you for having my daughter at your house."

"It was a pleasure. And thank you for *your* invitation," Mrs. B. said.

"We will see you soon," said MaMá.

"Come again to play, cutie-pie." Mrs. B. waved one last time before she closed the door.

MaMá led Ginny to the sidewalk. "You said your friend was Chinese," she said.

"She *is*. You've seen her."

"Not the same. She is not raised as a Chinese. Look how everyone wears dirty shoes in the house."

"But they like Chinese things. Mrs. B. liked the steamed buns," Ginny said.

"Hmph." MaMá sniffed and let out her breath in a white puff.

They walked on, their footsteps loud in the frosty night.

Ginny squeezed MaMá's hand. "Why doesn't Stephanie look like her parents?"

"She is adopted, Ah Mei."

"Adopted?"

"It means that they are taking care of her like they are her real parents. They signed papers."

"Where are her real parents?"

"That is not our business, Ah Mei."

Ginny walked down a straight line where

squares joined together in the sidewalk. She had to walk straight while she took all this in. "But don't you want to know, MaMá?"

"It is better not to know, Ah Mei."

Ginny walked quietly beside MaMá, holding her hand tight. "What did Stephanie's mom mean when she said thank you for inviting her?"

"I invited them to BaBá's party. Now stop asking so many questions." MaMá pulled a tissue from her pocket and wiped her nose.

They walked the rest of the way in silence, stepping carefully around the patches of ice.

"At Stephanie's house, they have Kool-Aid and white bread. She has a room full of toys."

MaMá listened quietly as they set out the place mats and the glasses with the silver spirals down the sides.

"At Stephanie's house, they have a TV in each room. The kitchen too."

Even as Ginny spoke, a shadow seemed to drift behind each sentence. Stephanie hadn't meant to share those things with her.

When Ginny finished folding the napkins, MaMá said, "Your friend may have all those things, Ah Mei, but you have your real Chinese parents."

Ginny was laying down MaMá's napkin. For a moment, she held on to the rectangle of paper. MaMá was right. What if Ginny had never known MaMá at all? What if she'd lived here in Virginia with white people while MaMá and Daddy still lived in China? She could hardly imagine such a thing.

Chapter Six

MaMá tucked her grocery list into her purse. The list was written in Chinese characters. "Good. We did not forget anything. We even got—what is that green stuff called?" She gestured with her fingers.

"Parsley." Ginny was pushing the shopping cart through the parking lot of Food Shoppers' Warehouse.

"Right. Parsley."

Just then, Ginny saw Stephanie and Mrs. B. leaving Craft Designs. "Look, MaMá!" she said.

She was about to wave, but then Robin came out the door too. Ginny dropped her hand.

"Hello, Ginny, Mrs. Liao," Mrs. B. called. "We were just going to get ice cream. Would you like to join us? My treat."

"We better not," MaMá said, looking at the shopping cart full of food.

"No, please. It'll be fun. We won't be long," Mrs. B. insisted.

Behind her, Stephanie and Robin were looking into a bag. They had identical barrettes in their ponytails, the kind with long ribbons streaming off them.

Ginny put her hand on MaMá's arm—*please?*

"Okay. For a little bit. But I do not want the food to go bad."

"Let's help you get it into the car. Stephanie, Robin! Come!" Mrs. B. grabbed a bag.

They unloaded the bags, bok choy and celery sticking out of the top.

"Looks like you're planning a Chinese feast," said Mrs. B.

MaMá smiled. She was going to cook the way she cooked every night.

Stephanie and Robin skipped ahead to Ice Cream Heaven. "Come on, Ginny," Stephanie shouted.

Ginny ran, turning to see Mrs. B. walking in her high heels beside MaMá, making MaMá look very small.

Robin ordered pistachio crunch, Stephanie rainbow sherbet. Ginny ordered rainbow sherbet too. Mrs. B. had a scoop of chocolate in a cone, MaMá vanilla in a cup.

Mrs. B. and MaMá sat together at one table.

"Here, Ginny," said Robin, patting a chair next to her. Robin's eyes were very blue.

Ginny licked the sherbet, sweet and cold, until her tongue felt frozen. Maybe Mrs. B. would invite her over to play with Stephanie and Robin.

Ginny noticed that MaMá kept looking around in her purse. She only took two bites of ice cream.

Mrs. B. opened the bag from Craft Designs. "Stephanie, give Ginny some of the embroidery thread we just bought. She'll probably want to join in the fun too."

Stephanie lifted out a handful of thick bright thread.

Ginny reached for the thread, then drew her hand back a little. It was string the girls used to make friendship bracelets.

She looked from Stephanie's face to Robin's. Were they planning to make friendship bracelets together?

Stephanie tucked the thread into Ginny's hand.

"What do you say?" said MaMá.

"Thank you, Mrs. B. Thank you, Stephanie."

Mrs. B. finished the last bite of her cone and got up, saying, "Well, I have to run Robin home now. I'll see you both at your Christmas party."

Mrs. B. wouldn't invite Ginny home after all. Suddenly, the rainbow sherbet seemed too sweet.

"Why are you so sad, Ah Mei?" MaMá asked as they walked to the car. "Was your ice cream not good?"

Ginny shook her head. "It wasn't that, MaMá."

"Did your friend make you sad?"

Ginny nodded. "I think she and Robin are best friends."

"Maybe you will get to know Stephanie better at BaBá's party," said MaMá, opening the car door for Ginny.

Ginny smiled a little. Robin wasn't invited. Ginny would have Stephanie all to herself.

Chapter Seven

"Daddy, Daddy! I got all pluses on my report card!"

He put down his suitcase, and Ginny threw herself into his arms, pressing her face against his coat, cold with melting snowflakes.

"Ah Mei, I bet you are the smartest second-grader in the world!" Whenever Daddy said her name, it sounded as if he really meant *Beautiful Little Heart.*

When they let go of each other, Ginny handed Daddy a paper Christmas tree. "I made this for you."

"I love it, Ah Mei," he said, holding up the tree, the glitter falling off like bright snow. "I'll hang it up in my office along with your paper Santa Claus." Daddy swung her up in the air. "I hope this Santa person isn't taking all your love away from me!"

Ginny laughed.

"I have something for you too." He set her down, opened his suitcase, and pulled out a box wrapped with gold paper and a pink bow.

Ginny opened the box to find the most beautiful dress she'd ever seen—pink and fluffy with blue ribbon trim. It was almost like the dress she'd seen in Stephanie's closet. "Oh, Daddy, can I wear it to the party?" she asked, holding the dress close and twirling around.

"Of course, Ah Mei."

She twirled one more time. She and Stephanie would be twins at Daddy's party.

Ginny lay on MaMá's bed, watching her at her vanity. She held her breath when MaMá picked up the false eyelashes with her long red finger-nails and glued them onto her eyelids. Then she blinked quickly, making sure the eyelashes were stuck tight.

MaMá caught Ginny's eye in the mirror and smiled as she buttoned the soft, loopy buttons of her red silk cheongsam. Then she swiveled the vanity stool to face Ginny. "And now, Ah Mei, it is time for you to get dressed." MaMá went into her walk-in closet and brought out Ginny's own cheongsam on its hanger.

A Chinese tailor had made it for Ginny's seventh birthday. She loved the high collar and tiny black flowers embroidered on the red silk.

But tonight she had something even better. She sat up on the bed. "I'm going to wear Daddy's new present. He already said I could."

"No pink dress tonight, Ah Mei. Many important people are coming."

"But the dress Daddy bought is really pretty."

"It is not Chinese, Ah Mei."

"I don't care. Stephanie has a pink holiday dress. And I want to wear a pink dress too. I won't wear that red thing." Ginny turned over on the bed, facing away from MaMá. Everything looked blurry through her tears.

"You will wear the cheongsam, Ah Mei."

Just then, Daddy walked into the room, his step quick as he crossed the carpet.

Daddy would be able to talk sense into MaMá.

But before Ginny could ask him, MaMá put her hands on her hips and announced, "Ah Mei wants to wear that dress you gave her. She must wear the cheongsam instead."

Daddy sat down beside Ginny, and she rolled a little toward him as the bed dipped. "MaMá is right, Ah Mei. Wear the cheongsam. There will be other times to wear the pink dress." Daddy whispered in her ear, "Be a good girl and listen to your *mamá.*"

Ginny couldn't believe that Daddy was taking MaMá's side! Didn't they know how hard it was to get a best friend? Ginny lay facedown on the bed and wouldn't look at either of them.

Chapter Eight

The green Chinese broccoli and the roasted red pork cutlets reminded Ginny of Christmas colors. Triangles of fried wontons bulged with cream cheese and lobster meat, and curly pink shrimp floated in a brown sauce with straw mushrooms like little hats. The baby corn was the perfect size for a doll. MaMá had drawn zigzaggy patterns with sauce over the spring rolls that Ginny had helped fill with lettuce, mint, and thin rice noodles.

The doorbell rang, and Ginny peeked out to

see Mrs. B.'s car. Her heart did a somersault. They had come!

Ginny thought of running upstairs and changing into her pink dress in spite of MaMá. Robin's mother wouldn't make *her* wear a cheongsam!

MaMá checked her hair in the hallway mirror before opening the door.

Stephanie was wearing her pink dress with tiny white dots. It didn't have sleeves, so she wore long white gloves just like a Cinderella Barbie. She glanced at Ginny's red cheongsam.

Ginny looked down so Stephanie wouldn't see her face, now red as the cheongsam. "I have a new pink dress. Just like yours. But my mom made me wear this," she whispered.

Mrs. B. leaned over and kissed Ginny's forehead. "Merry Christmas, honey. I just love your outfit. I wish that Stephanie would wear something like that. You look like a little China doll."

China doll? She didn't want to be a China doll. She wanted to be a Cinderella Barbie.

MaMá pulled a red envelope from her pocket. She handed the *lai-see* to Stephanie. "I hope you like it."

Stephanie turned the envelope over as though she didn't know what was inside.

How could she be Chinese and not know about *lai-see*?

It was impolite to open a gift in front of others. But Stephanie had American parents and didn't have to follow Chinese rules. "Open it," Ginny told her.

Stephanie peeked in and smiled. "Oh thanks, Mrs. Liao!"

Ginny glimpsed the corner of a twenty-dollar bill.

"In the Chinese culture, that is lucky money," MaMá said. "Make sure your mother puts that in your bank account." She gestured toward the door that led into the other room.

"Well, this is certainly a feast." Mrs. B. looked over the mountains of food.

The doorbell rang again and again. Daddy's friends arrived with enchiladas, noodle salads, chocolate brownies dotted with nuts, and cookies shaped like reindeer.

MaMá kept rearranging the unfamiliar foods on the table. "Ah Mei, move that here." And "Ah Mei, move that there."

"What is that name your mom calls you?" Stephanie asked.

"It's my Chinese name. It's short for Xin Mei."

"So you have two names?"

Ginny nodded. "One for school, one for home."

When all the guests had come, Daddy, wearing his tie with the dancing Santas, pulled out chairs for Mrs. B. and Stephanie.

"Eat, everyone," MaMá called out. "Please do not be shy. Eat."

Ginny bit into a reindeer cookie.

Stephanie took off the long white gloves, and right away, Ginny saw that she wore a green-and-purple friendship bracelet on her left wrist. It had to be Robin's friendship bracelet.

Her bite of cookie went down the wrong way. She coughed and had to drink some water.

"This is a real treat. I only cook simple things myself," Mrs. B. said, taking the dish of broccoli. "If it weren't for Ragú spaghetti sauce, my family would starve."

"Here, Stephanie, try some of my fried rice." MaMá held up a plate. Her fried rice had peas and carrots, and most special of all, Chinese sausage. Everyone loved it.

Stephanie shook her head. "No, thanks."

"How about a spring roll?"

"I don't eat Chinese food, Mrs. Liao."

MaMá made her mouth tight. "Hmph."

What was wrong with Stephanie? Even Americans loved MaMá's food.

If Stephanie wouldn't eat Chinese food, Ginny wouldn't either. Instead, she ate green bean casserole, bundt cake, deviled eggs, and garlic bread.

"Ah Mei, you will become fat as that Santa person," said MaMá.

Stephanie giggled.

Ginny licked the garlicky butter from her fingers.

Mrs. B. put her hand on Stephanie's shoulder. "You really should try some of Mrs. Liao's delicious food."

Stephanie turned away and pointed to the glass cabinet. "What are those?"

Inside the cabinet paraded MaMá's twelve animals of the zodiac, including Ginny's dragon.

"Chinese people believe that you have an animal, depending on which year you were born in," Ginny said.

"Like a pet?"

Ginny wasn't sure about that, but she nodded anyway.

She'd always wanted to take the jade animals out and play with them, but MaMá had never let her.

"The dragon is Ah Mei's special animal," MaMá said. "When my husband and I first came to America, we brought a piece of jade. Ah Mei was born in the year of the dragon. When she was one month old her *babá* had the jade carved into the shape of a dragon."

"What an interesting story," said Mrs. B.

"Ooooohhh." Stephanie got out of her chair and went to the glass case. "How cute they all are. The green stone is so shiny and pretty."

"That's called jade, sweetheart," said Mrs. B.

Ginny pointed to the dragon at the front of the

case. "My mom says that because that's my animal, I am very powerful."

"Really?" Stephanie asked.

"Really." Ginny said. "You too, Stephanie. You were born in the same year. The dragon is your animal too."

"You know that, Stephanie," said Mr. B. "Remember how we found your year on the place mat at Peking Gourmet?"

Ginny looked more closely than usual at the dragon. It stood so proudly among the other animals. It was *their* animal, hers and Stephanie's, something that linked them together.

Stephanie touched the glass case. "Ginny, can I hold the dragon?"

"Well . . ." Ginny said.

Mrs. B. leaned forward and took Stephanie's hand. "No, sweetheart. Don't ask Ginny something like that. That dragon is too valuable. Come sit down. Believe it or not, more food is coming."

Chapter Nine

Ginny and Stephanie went up to Ginny's bedroom to play. Her room had a bed, a dresser, and a desk. No canopy. No TV.

Stephanie looked around. "Where are your toys?"

"That's all I have." Ginny gestured toward the Etch A Sketch, the box of paint-by-number canvases with their tiny containers of paint, and a Mr. Potato Head. "My parents think toys are silly."

"Doesn't Santa bring you any?"

"Not yet." Ginny rocked from one foot to the other. "Maybe this year."

Stephanie glanced toward the closet.

There, between the winter coats and school dresses, hung Daddy's pink dress with the blue trim. "This is it, Stephanie." Ginny lifted the skirt of the dress. "We would have been so pretty together."

"Too bad your mom made you wear that instead." Stephanie glanced again at Ginny's cheongsam.

"I wanted to wear my pink dress like you. I wanted us to be twins." Ginny pulled Stephanie by the arm, so that they stood in front of the mirror: two girls the same height with straight black hair, eyes like crescent moons, and clear round faces. They smiled at each other in the glass.

Stephanie sat down in the desk chair. She opened the desk drawer and fingered Ginny's neat row of colored pencils. She began to tap her toes on the carpet. "Now what?" she asked.

Ginny looked around the bare room. Stephanie had to have fun. "Do you want to draw something?"

"Not really. I'm not in the mood."

What would Stephanie like? She couldn't let her be bored. Robin had made her a friendship bracelet. "How about if we play Go Fish?"

"That's a baby game."

Ginny stared at the window and the black night outside. If only Santa would appear with a bag full of toys.

"Does your mom ever let you play with those little animals downstairs?" Stephanie asked.

"Never," Ginny said firmly.

"They're cute. Especially the dragon." Stephanie took out the colored pencils and a piece of paper and began to draw one of her blond princesses.

Ginny sat down on the bed. She should have made Stephanie a friendship bracelet.

Stephanie moved the yellow pencil more slowly, as if she was about to lay it down. Then what?

It couldn't hurt to borrow just one animal. Just for a little while. Maybe not the dragon. Maybe the rat, or the rooster.

But it was the dragon that Stephanie had mentioned. It was their animal. "How about if we bring the dragon up here for a few minutes?" Ginny asked.

"Really?" Stephanie looked up. "Could I hold it?"

Everyone was eating dessert in the living room. It was easy for Ginny and Stephanie to slip into the dining room and open the glass case.

Ginny put her hand on the dragon, the stone smooth and cool, the scales sharp. Green fire curled out of the mouth.

They had to be quick. Ginny pushed the other animals around so that MaMá wouldn't notice the hole. "You can't tell anyone. This is our secret."

Ginny put the dragon into Stephanie's hands, and they dashed upstairs.

Back in Ginny's room, with the door closed, Stephanie whispered, "Can I take it home?"

Ginny shook her head. "Oh, no, Stephanie. My mom would miss it for sure."

Stephanie set the dragon on Ginny's desk and turned it this way and that, looking at it from all angles. Then she held the cool jade to her cheek.

"Do you really want to take it overnight?" Ginny asked.

"You mean for a toy slumber party?" Stephanie put the dragon in her lap, nestled in the pink nylon of her dress.

Ginny nodded.

"What about your mom?"

Ginny grew cold all over at the mention of

MaMá, but said, "It's okay. She doesn't really look at the animals that often."

When everyone had gone, Daddy rolled up his sleeves, took off his tie and shoes, and lay back in his recliner. "Ah Mei, tell your *mamá* to relax. She needs to kick up her feet and pat herself on the back."

MaMá put her hands on her hips. "What are you saying? Liao Kai, you are sounding more and more American every day. What is this silly talk, kicking and patting? I am too tired to kick and pat."

Ginny tried not to look at the glass case. The animals were staring back at her, asking, *Where is our sister?*

When Stephanie had said good-bye, she'd given Ginny a hug. "This is such a cool toy," she'd said, patting her coat pocket. "It's our secret."

"Did you have fun with your little friend?" Daddy asked.

"Yes, Daddy."

MaMá sat down on Daddy's lap. "That girl did not like my food. Chinese should eat Chinese food. Chinese should know their culture."

"Her face may be Chinese, but her mind is American," said Daddy. He reached out his arm and brought Ginny close to him on the arm of the chair. "Our Ah Mei is Chinese through and through."

As Ginny snuggled against Daddy, she wondered how she could be Chinese through and through when she'd given away her Chinese dragon.

Chapter Ten

"Do you want to see our Christmas tree, Ginny?" Stephanie said on Saturday morning.

"Oh, yes, Stephanie, yes." Ginny clutched the pink phone. "I'd love to."

Stephanie's voice grew soft. "You can also visit our little secret."

Our little secret. Ginny remembered the dragon. She shivered, wishing the secret was not *that* secret.

When Ginny arrived, she found a tree that almost touched the ceiling of Stephanie's living room. There was just space for the angel on top, her wings folded as if she would stay forever. Chains of tinsel looped through the branches.

"These aren't Santa presents." Stephanie waved at the boxes piled under the tree. "These are from my mom and dad." She pointed to a box wrapped in glittery foil. "And this is from Grandma Nancy. This one is Uncle Hunter's. Santa's presents will come later. To make sure that Santa comes to your house, you have to put out milk and cookies. If you do that, he'll bring exactly what you want."

Stephanie moved the presents aside.

When Ginny lay down, she looked up into the lights reflecting the shiny ornaments.

"Listen," Stephanie said, picking up a little

Santa riding a sleigh. She wound a key on the Santa's back. The toy began to play "Jingle Bells" in time to the blinking lights.

Ginny wanted to lie gazing up into the needly branches forever. She wanted to breathe in the piney smell forever. But her dragon was here at Stephanie's house. She had to know it was safe. "Can we go upstairs now?" she asked.

Red-and-green ribbons wound around the banister on the staircase, making it look like a giant candy cane.

Stephanie's room was decorated with lights around the edge of her canopy bed and fir branches with red bows on her dresser.

But Ginny hardly looked at the decorations. She had to find the dragon.

It lay in a doll bed with the covers over it. She lifted the covers. The poor dragon was wrapped up like a baby. When it had lived in the glass case, it had looked like a royal beast. Now it was a toy baby.

Oh, no. Ginny had no idea Stephanie would treat her dragon like this. The dragon was their power animal.

But Ginny looked at Stephanie and at her room full of toys, and covered the dragon again.

"Let's play dolls," Stephanie said. "You be this one." She handed a doll with curly blond hair to Ginny. "Let's pretend that the dolls are going to a party. I'll be this other one."

Ginny made the doll skate across the carpet.

"She can't go to the party in *that* outfit. Here." Stephanie picked up a white party dress and threw it toward Ginny. "And you gotta take off her roller skates sometime, Ginny, or her legs will get tired."

Ginny changed the doll's dress and took off her skates and put tiny high heels on her. She kept her eye on the dragon lying in the doll bed.

At the same time, she didn't want to look at it at all.

Stephanie got the dragon out of the bed and unwrapped it. She put a ribbon around its neck like a leash. She placed one end of the leash in the doll's hand. "Look, Ginny. Just like a little dog."

Ginny bit her lip.

"I want to keep the dragon longer. I'll trade you something for it," Stephanie said.

"Well . . ." Ginny hesitated. Someday MaMá would notice the missing dragon. When she did, she would yell and scream.

But Stephanie was holding the dragon in both hands.

Stephanie pulled out one drawer after another. "How about this?" She held out a ring. It had a big pink diamond in the center, with little white diamonds around it. "My grandma gave it to me. It's one of the most special things I own."

She slipped it onto her finger and sighed. "But you can borrow it."

Ginny put it on her own finger and held her hand up to the light. The ring glittered. It would match her pink dress. "Thank you, Stephanie."

Stephanie's ring was even better than a friendship bracelet.

Then Ginny took off the ring and put it in her pocket. MaMá must never ever see it.

Chapter Eleven

"MaMá, where are the cookies from Daddy's party?"

"I threw them away. They are not good for you."

Ginny looked in the refrigerator. "Where's the milk?"

"We do not have any. Do not spoil your appetite, Ah Mei."

Stephanie had said milk and cookies. If there weren't any, Santa might not come. Ginny sat down at the kitchen table and laid her head on her folded arms. "It's not for me. It's for Santa."

"I do not understand you, Ah Mei." MaMá came and stood behind her. Her voice softened. "I have some almond cookies in the pantry and soybean milk in the case on the floor."

On Christmas morning, Ginny crept down to the living room.

The presents on the coffee table were wrapped as though Santa had brought them. Ginny thought of the letter she'd sent, and a flicker of excitement shot up her spine. She would have a doll just like Stephanie's.

She untied a gold bow and let the red paper fall away to reveal a package of white socks.

The next present was a pack of pencils. Not even Christmas pencils with red and green designs, but yellow number-two pencils with pink erasers.

Ginny felt through the wrapping paper of the packages, looking for the hard outline of a doll box. But she felt only what turned out to be a pair of flannel pajamas. A package of underwear.

No doll.

And then she realized that the glass of soybean milk and the plate of almond cookies she'd set out were still in front of the mantelpiece, untouched.

Socks. Underwear. A pair of pajamas. Pencils.

Suddenly, she knew that MaMá had given her those things. That it hadn't been Santa. Santa hadn't come, even though she'd written him a letter. Even though Daddy had checked the roof.

Santa didn't come to Chinese kids. She'd left out almond cookies and soybean milk. Santa didn't like that kind of food.

Socks. Underwear. A pair of pajamas. Pencils.

Santa hadn't come. She'd known all along that he wouldn't.

Then Ginny had a worse thought, the worst

thought ever. *Santa hadn't come because she'd stolen the jade dragon for Stephanie.*

Ginny went upstairs and climbed back into bed. As she lay with the covers pulled over her head, she wondered if Ricky had gotten his light saber, if Santa had brought Robin a Princess Leia doll.

Chapter Twelve

After winter break, Stephanie began to chase Ricky again as usual.

"Help me, Ginny," she called out. "Don't just stand there."

Ginny tore across the playground. Her shoes had little high heels and her toes were shoved into the pointy toes, but she ran fast and didn't care. The two of them chased Ricky in and out of the monkey bars.

She caught Ricky by the sleeve of his jacket. He twisted, but no way would she let him loose.

"Good job, Ginny," Stephanie said.

Ginny took Ricky by one arm and Stephanie took the other. They sang the song together. "We go together. . . . Chang-chang changity-chang shoo-bop. . . ." Yes, finally they were *all* going together.

Even her. Ginny sang as loud as she could.

Every Saturday, Ginny went to Stephanie's. Together, they watched *Fat Albert* cartoons, with the characters Mushmouth and the Brown Hornet; ate bacon and grits—delicious ground-up corn with pats of butter; and built a snowman with a carrot nose.

At school, they spent every recess together. Instead of playing *Grease,* they played *Star Wars.* They took turns at being Princess Leia, braiding and coiling each other's hair.

"Look, Stephanie. The monkey bars make a starship!" Ginny said.

Sometimes Ricky, carrying his new Christmas light saber, was Luke Skywalker, sometimes Darth Vader.

One morning, Stephanie held something behind her back. "Which hand?"

Ginny pointed to her right.

"Nope," Stephanie said. "But you can have it anyway." She handed Ginny a necklace chain. On it hung a heart—no, half a heart.

Half a heart?

"Surprise!" Stephanie pulled another chain from underneath her blouse. She wore a half-heart necklace too. "Together, we have one whole heart."

"We go together, don't we?" Ginny gave Stephanie a big hug.

Stephanie said, "Like peanut butter and jelly."

Ginny laughed. "Like egg and roll."

They would be best friends forever.

Chapter Thirteen

When Ginny showed MaMá the necklace, she said, "It is broken."

"No, it's not. Stephanie has the other half. It means we're best friends."

MaMá smiled a funny smile. "Okay. Nice."

"MaMá, Stephanie invited me to spend the night with her on Saturday."

MaMá was cleaning the furniture, spraying the lemon polish on, then wiping it off, moving her cloth in circles. "I do not want you to be at Stephanie's house so much, Ah Mei."

"Why can't I go, MaMá? I've never spent the night with a friend."

"You need to be more with your family. BaBá will be home this weekend." MaMá finished with the polish and began to straighten a row of silver cushions on the couch.

But Ginny just had to go to Stephanie's. No one had ever invited her for a sleepover. How could she get MaMá to say yes? Pleading with MaMá wouldn't work. Ginny thought and thought until she came up with a plan.

On purpose, she got a bad grade on her math test the next day.

"Aren't you feeling well, Ginny?" Mrs. Vincent asked.

When Ginny brought the test home, MaMá held it up to the light, studying it. "Why did you not do good, Ah Mei?"

Ginny shook her head, as if confused. "The

numbers are getting so big, MaMá. I don't understand about borrowing. Especially if there's a zero."

"Well, I can teach you about that. Sit down."

MaMá took out her abacus, her special Chinese counting tool. "Like this." She moved the beads back and forth on the wires.

Ginny heard those beads at the end of the month when MaMá paid the bills. When MaMá paid the bills, she locked her teeth together and muttered angry Chinese words.

Ginny sank her chin into her hands. "I don't get it, MaMá."

"But it is very simple, Ah Mei."

"But that's not how my teacher does it. She writes everything on the chalkboard."

"That is the American way. The Chinese way is better. This"—she picked up the abacus with both hands—"can help with the mathematics that is so hard that even your teacher cannot do it on the board."

"But MaMá!" Ginny's voice filled the kitchen. "Nobody in my class uses an abacus. I don't want to use it." She crossed her arms and turned her head to the side.

"I do not know what to do with you, Ah Mei." MaMá pushed the abacus away. "You are so spoiled. American kids have no respect. When I was little, I always listened to my parents. You do not want to learn? You will get bad grades and then you will not be able to go to college and you will work at McDonald's. Do not come home to me. I will not take care of you anymore."

Ginny almost smiled. Sometimes MaMá talked so crazy.

But the moment had come. "You know, MaMá, Stephanie always gets 100 percent on her math tests." Ginny said it as though it weren't important, as though she were just chatting.

"That is because she is Chinese. She is smart."

"I just don't understand take-aways, but

Stephanie does." Ginny dropped her chin into her hands.

"Do you think Stephanie can help you with your take-aways?"

"Of course, MaMá. Stephanie is a good teacher."

"Hmm," said MaMá.

"If I go to her house overnight, I promise we'll do our homework first."

"No playing around?" asked MaMá, looking into Ginny's eyes.

Ginny shook her head. "Just math."

"Should I pay her? How much? We do not want to owe anybody." MaMá pulled the abacus close again and slid the beads. "Let's see . . . each hour at . . ."

Ginny had to think fast. MaMá mustn't offer money to Stephanie. "She is having trouble with grammar. So we'll trade. She already asked me to help her."

Ginny waited, her heart sliding back and forth like MaMá's beads.

"Trading is okay. But no begging. You are not a beggar."

"I promise to trade, MaMá." Again, Ginny waited.

"Okay. You may go to Stephanie's. But only to study mathematics. Not to play with silly toys."

"Oh, thank you, MaMá." Ginny felt a flash of guilt. How could she trick MaMá like this? Yet it was MaMá's fault for not letting her go in the first place. Ginny ran upstairs to pack her overnight bag.

Chapter Fourteen

"All right, girls. Teeth brushed? Hair combed? Pajamas on?" Mrs. B. came into the room with her hands on her hips.

"Check. Check. Check." Stephanie drew imaginary check marks in the air with her finger.

"Good. Under the sheets you two go." Mrs. B. lifted the pink sheets.

Ginny lay down and stared up into the canopy with its fringe of tassels. The print on the ceiling of the canopy matched the print of the comforter—sprigs of purple flowers that seemed to dance across the fabric.

As Mrs. B. lowered the panels of the canopy, she asked, "Bedtime story tonight, or not?"

"Not tonight, Mommy," Stephanie answered. "Ginny and I have things to talk about."

"Don't stay up too late. You need your beauty sleep."

Ginny heard her kiss Stephanie's cheek. Then she felt Mrs. B.'s soft, warm lips on her own forehead. She squeezed her eyes tight. MaMá never kissed her.

"Good night, darlings." Mrs. B. turned off the lights. "Sleep tight. Don't let the bedbugs bite." She closed the door.

When Mrs. B.'s footsteps had died away, Stephanie whispered, "Tell me a secret."

"What kind of secret?" Ginny had only one secret. The stolen dragon was here in the room with them, taking a bath in the dollhouse bathtub—a secret she didn't want to think about.

"Any kind. Something that you don't want anyone to know."

Ginny snuggled deeper under the soft, puffy comforter. A night-light shaped like a whale cast a soft blue glow in the room.

"How about telling me a secret thought or feeling?"

Ginny searched her mind. Nothing. Nothing at all. She pressed the warm stone of Stephanie's ring to her cheek.

"Okay," said Stephanie, "I'll start." She took a big breath and whispered, as though she were on a stage, "Once I took a pack of gum from the market. I put it in my pocket when no one was looking."

Ginny shuddered in spite of the warm bed. MaMá would scream if she did anything like that. But then she remembered. "One time I took my mom's fake eyelashes. I tried to put them on. I covered them with white glue and ruined them."

Stephanie giggled.

The Sleeping Beauty clock ticked on, as if nothing were happening. First Ginny yawned, then Stephanie.

"Ginny," came Stephanie's voice, very low. "I have another secret. Cross your heart like this." Stephanie drew an *X* over her chest with her fingertips. "That means you promise not to tell."

Ginny crossed her heart.

Stephanie scooted close to Ginny.

Ginny could smell the minty toothpaste smell of her breath.

"Okay. Here goes. Sometimes I wish my parents were Chinese."

Ginny's eyes flew open. "You *do*?"

"Then everyone wouldn't stare at us."

Ginny lay frozen, not even blinking.

"Or sometimes"—Stephanie moved closer so that her lips were practically against Ginny's cheek—"I just wish they'd left me in China."

"Oh," Ginny breathed. This *was* a secret. Ginny crossed her heart again.

"You think it's hard to be different from kids at school. Just imagine being different from your own mother and father."

Ginny nodded, her head making a rustling sound against the crisp pillowcase.

"Now your turn," Stephanie said suddenly and brightly.

Ginny had nothing to match Stephanie's secret. She pulled the comforter higher over her shoulders. What could she offer? She felt Stephanie waiting. She searched for what Stephanie wanted to hear. Finally, she found it.

She whispered, "Sometimes I wish I wasn't Chinese."

"What? What did you say?" Stephanie edged closer.

On the other side of the gauzy panels of the canopy, the eyes of the hundreds of dolls and stuffed animals seemed to be watching, the ears cocked to listen.

"Cross your heart," Ginny ordered.

Stephanie lifted her arm high and drew a big cross in the air above her heart.

"I wish I was just American," Ginny said quietly.

The minute she'd said it, she wished she hadn't. She wished she could pull the words right out of the air. They seemed to hang there for anyone to hear. How would MaMá and Daddy feel to hear those words?

She glanced toward the listening toys, vague beyond the filmy fabric.

"Wow," Stephanie said. "I never would have guessed. That's a big secret." Stephanie flipped onto her back and gazed up into the canopy.

Ginny watched Stephanie's profile, backlit by the bluish light.

Stephanie leaned up on one elbow. "But what about your whole Chinese life? The food and all?" she asked. "I thought you liked all that."

"I do. Just sometimes . . ."

". . . you wish . . ." Stephanie said.

Ginny nodded. She couldn't say the words again.

"That's my secret too," Stephanie said, lying back down. "Even more than my parents being Chinese, I wish we were all white." She reached for Ginny's hand, fumbling under the comforter. When she found it, she locked her fingers through Ginny's and they both squeezed.

"Sometimes I don't even like to see Chinese people," Stephanie continued. "When I see them, I think of my real parents."

Ginny gave Stephanie's hand a squeeze. She closed her eyes. Suddenly, she felt very sleepy again and not like sharing any more secrets. She heard Stephanie's breathing deepen and soften.

Then Stephanie said sleepily, as though she were talking from a dream, "I wish I had a Chinese name like you."

Ginny opened her eyes again. "You *do*?"

"Just kidding. I already have a name."

Ginny laughed, as though Stephanie were being funny. She closed her eyes again. As if in a dream herself, she said, "One time in kindergarten, MaMá called me, using my Chinese name. All the kids started singing, *"Ching chong ching."*

Stephanie let go of Ginny's hand, and sat up. "Even without a Chinese name, they do that. I hate it. I really hate it! When I was in first grade—"

A tap came on the door. "Girls. Time for sleeping. Quiet, please."

Stephanie lay back down, her eyes wide open. Ginny's eyes were wide open too.

They lay side by side. *Tick, tock.* Ginny thought

about searching out Stephanie's hand, but didn't. Even though she and Stephanie lay so close that their bare feet touched and their minty breath mingled, they were apart now, lost in their own secrets.

Chapter Fifteen

The next morning, Ginny and Stephanie were watching *Bugs Bunny*. Elmer Fudd was chasing Bugs with a big frying pan.

"He wants to cook him!" Stephanie exclaimed.

They lay in their pajamas, watching the TV upside down, their feet on the back of the couch. They'd been braiding friendship bracelets and barrettes with long streamers. Embroidery thread and ribbons lay strewn over the couch.

"See if you can eat popcorn without sitting up," said Stephanie.

Ginny took a handful from the bucket and was stuffing it into her mouth, when she saw MaMá standing behind the couch.

Elmer Fudd hit Bugs—*whack, whack*—over the head with the frying pan.

Mrs. B. stood behind MaMá, a big smile on her face.

MaMá was not smiling. "Where are the mathematics books?" she asked.

Ginny sat up and swallowed the popcorn without chewing it. She felt the scratchy kernels in her throat. "We studied already, MaMá."

"So Stephanie has already taught you your take-aways?"

"Yes, MaMá."

"What?" asked Stephanie. "We didn't have any homework, did we?"

Ginny made a face at Stephanie, but Stephanie only shrugged.

"Get your things, Ah Mei," MaMá said.

Mrs. B. lifted up the bucket of popcorn, as if to offer some to MaMá. "Ginny has been a perfect little houseguest. No trouble at all."

On the way home, MaMá said, "You lied to me, Ah Mei."

Ginny hung her head and scuffed at a pile of dead leaves.

"If you keep behaving like this, Ah Mei," MaMá continued, "I will have to send you to China to learn respect for your parents. Real Chinese girls would never lie. I will send you to a school in China."

Ginny's lower lip quivered. *China!* She'd seen China on maps—a big tan flat space. It didn't seem to have green trees, or buildings, or houses, or cars. Just tan. How could anyone live in a place that looked like the newsprint drawing paper at school?

When the cafeteria monitor wanted kids to

eat their food, she said children were starving in China. Ginny didn't want to starve.

"I don't want to go to China, MaMá." Ginny bit her lower lip to keep it from trembling.

"Then no more tricking me."

"No, MaMá. I promise." Yet she was tricking MaMá even now. Right this moment even. She thought of the dragon in the dollhouse bathtub.

In Chinese, MaMá asked Ginny to get her something, but Ginny didn't understand what.

"Ah Mei! Are you listening? Do it now." MaMá pointed toward the drawer. Was she asking for a spoon or a napkin or a knife?

"MaMá, I don't know what you're saying. What do you want me to get? Please say it in English."

"Never mind." MaMá opened a drawer and got out the place mats. "You have forgotten your Chinese."

Ginny set out a place mat for MaMá and one for herself.

"You have been visiting that girl Stephanie too much. Watching those silly cartoons. That girl has no Chinese culture."

"Stephanie is my best friend and . . ." *And a dragon, just like me,* Ginny almost said. But she didn't dare mention dragons in front of MaMá.

Chapter Sixteen

When MaMá pulled into the parking lot at Annandale High School, the snow on the ground and falling in the air made everyone's black hair look even blacker. Through the falling snow, Ginny heard only Chinese words.

She had always looked for Chinese faces, and now everyone was Chinese. These kids, she realized, wouldn't say *"ching chong"* or pull at the edges of their eyes.

Here she would learn calligraphy, just as MaMá had promised.

MaMá took Ginny's hand and led her into the tall brick building. Inside a booth, a sign read REGISTRATION in English underneath the Chinese characters.

MaMá filled out papers, writing in Chinese. The only characters Ginny could read were those of her formal Chinese name: *Liao Xin Mei.*

"Ah Mei, your Chinese teacher will be Mrs. Chang." MaMá pointed to a tall lady with glasses and a black bun. "All the Chinese people in Fairfax County come here to learn Chinese language and culture," MaMá said. "Be a good girl and study hard. I will wait for you in the cafeteria."

MaMá walked Ginny to room 1004 and waved good-bye.

Ginny stood in the doorway, watching the teacher hang posters of Chinese characters over the American school posters. She smiled.

Other children began to come in, chatting

away in Chinese. Ginny could hardly understand what they were saying.

When the teacher said *Xin Mei,* Ginny guessed that she was introducing her.

The class greeted her in unison: *"Zaoshang hao."*

Everyone opened their books. The books had pictures of Chinese people. Ginny never saw Chinese people in the books at her American school. The kids began to read out loud. Ginny pretended to read too, moving her lips, but with no sound coming out.

Ginny thought of the way she liked to play detective with the characters in MaMá's newspaper. But here, reading was no game. The other kids knew how to read, and it even looked easy for them.

A voice came on the loudspeaker and announced—first in Chinese and then in English—that it was time to change classes.

When the other children went out to the hallway, Ginny sat by herself, staring at the book she couldn't read.

About this time, *The Smurfs* would be coming on TV. "La la la la la la . . ." she and Stephanie always sang along with the little blue people who lived in Smurf Village.

Ginny ran her thumb over her heart necklace. She hoped that Stephanie was missing her too, maybe even touching her own heart necklace.

With her fingertips, Ginny wiped the edges of her eyes.

Then Mrs. Chang said, "*Zai jian,* Xin Mei. Good-bye."

Ginny stood up.

Mrs. Chang beckoned her to the doorway. "Right there." She pointed out the door. "Your calligraphy class is in room 1006."

"*Zai jian,*" Ginny said, and walked down the hall.

"Hello, Xin Mei. I'm Miss Yee," said a lady with black hair cut in a bowl shape.

Miss Yee put a piece of paper on each desk— thin yellow paper with red lines that formed columns. Instead of brushes like MaMá's, Miss Yee handed out pencils.

Miss Yee wrote characters on the chalkboard, and beside them she wrote the English words. Then she came to Ginny. "Here is your name, Liao Xin Mei." She wrote the characters on a piece of plain white paper. "Now, copy this and the words on the board until you have them memorized."

Ginny pretended that her pencil was a brush like MaMá's.

Over and over, Ginny copied her name, and the words *mountain, tree,* and *river.* MaMá's song about the moon danced through her head. Ginny loved the characters, and just like at home, she made up stories about them: *This is a house with a river running by it. . . .* Soon she lost herself in the strokes.

When the voice announced the end of class, the kids got up and started out the door.

Ginny handed Miss Yee her Chinese writing paper.

Miss Yee held it a little away from her and studied it. "Xin Mei, this is beautiful. You have natural talent."

But when she gave the paper back to Ginny, she didn't put a red check mark on it or a stamp or a sticker. How would MaMá know that she had done good work?

Even before Ginny got to the cafeteria, she heard MaMá talking in Chinese and laughing loudly. As she came into the room, she saw MaMá playing mah-jongg with the other ladies, the little blocks with the green backs clicking against each other. MaMá must have told a joke because the others were laughing too. She waved her hands in the air. Not like the quiet MaMá of the ice-cream shop.

Ginny heard the words *Miss Fortmann* and knew that MaMá was telling the story of how Ginny had once spoken Chinese and now didn't.

The women's faces grew serious.

"And now I cannot talk to my own daughter in my own language," MaMá finished up in English as Ginny came close. "How was Chinese School?" MaMá asked.

Ginny smiled. "The teacher liked my calligraphy."

MaMá took Ginny's paper in both hands, then spoke in Chinese again to her new friends, pointing at the strokes.

She looked up at Ginny and said in English, "Your very first day of calligraphy, Ah Mei. And almost perfect! We'll hang this up on the refrigerator." She turned to her friends. "My silly girl is always wanting to put things on the refrigerator. These American-born Chinese!"

Ginny smiled again.

The phone rang several times before Stephanie answered. "I didn't hear it at first because the TV was on loud," she explained.

"I just got back from Chinese School, Stephanie. I liked it."

"You *liked* it?"

"Yeah, it was neat." Ginny sat down at the little table in the hallway. "I got to do calligraphy."

"What's calli—whatever?" Stephanie asked.

"It's special Chinese writing. It looks like art." Ginny twisted the curly phone cord around her finger. "Do you want to go with me next time?"

In the background, Ginny heard a cartoon coming on.

"Saturday morning is cartoon time." Over the top of the music, Stephanie said, "Ginny, remember what you told me when you slept over? The secret I promised never to tell?"

Ginny glanced around to make sure that MaMá was still unloading groceries in the kitchen. "Yeah?"

"Well, you said that you don't like to be—you know—and then you go off to Chinese School?"

Ginny rubbed her toe around and around in a circle on the beige carpet. "Yes?"

"So . . ."

Ginny sat up straight with both feet on the floor. "I liked the calligraphy. The calligraphy was fun."

"I bet not as fun as cartoons."

After Ginny had set the phone back on the cradle, she wondered if Stephanie would invite Robin to spend Saturdays with her.

One day at lunch, Stephanie asked, "Will you have to go to Chinese School *every* Saturday?" She peeled the lid off her Jell-O snack. "You've left me by myself two whole Saturdays."

"My mom says I have to go so I will be more Chinese."

"But you're already Chinese. Just look at your lunch."

Ginny stared down at her steamed rice and snow peas. Suddenly, she had a good idea. "This Saturday I don't have Chinese School. We're celebrating Chinese New Year. Stephanie, why don't you come with us?"

Stephanie finished her apple with big, quick bites and threw the core into her lunch box. "Maybe."

"MaMá, can I invite Stephanie to Chinese New Year with us?"

"Ah Mei, I am busy right now." MaMá was cleaning the house for Chinese New Year.

"Please, MaMá?"

"Ah Mei, she is not going to like Chinese New Year," said MaMá, leaning the mop against the wall. She reached for a jar of garlic sauce on the counter.

"But MaMá, Stephanie is my best friend in the whole world. Please, MaMá, please."

"Ah Mei, what am I going to do with you?" The buzzer on the dryer sounded. MaMá dropped the sauce, and the glass jar smashed onto the clean floor.

Ginny bent to pick up the broken glass. "Please, MaMá?"

The dryer buzzed again.

"Do not touch that glass, Ah Mei." With the mop, MaMá shoved the glass into the corner.

Ginny looked up at her.

"Do what you want." MaMá dropped the mop and ran downstairs to the laundry, muttering, "Stubborn girl."

Chapter Seventeen

"Gong Xi Fa Cai!"

Ginny opened her eyes to see Daddy at the foot of her bed.

As usual, Ginny reached under her pillow and found the *lai-see*. A brand-new one-hundred-dollar bill was tucked inside the red envelope.

But the money was not to spend. MaMá would take it to Ginny's bank account.

Daddy peeled the covers back and lifted Ginny up out of bed. He twirled her around, calling out,

"Happy Chinese New Year!" again, then carried her downstairs.

There were harvest moon cakes on the kitchen table, and chrysanthemum tea was brewing on the stovetop. MaMá had even made the little *dan-tat,* the egg custard pies that Ginny loved. She had bought sticky rice with pork sausage wrapped in banana leaves. Piled high on plates were steamed pork buns, which looked like big Hershey Kisses with a red dot on the top, and pineapple buns with crusts of yellow sugar, stuffed with sweet custard.

"Better than Christmas, right?" MaMá said, smiling as she loaded drinks into the picnic cooler.

"We have to pick up Stephanie, remember?"

"Ah Mei, this is our holiday. Americans don't understand it." MaMá shook her head as she closed the lid of the cooler.

"But MaMá, you already said that I could invite her. No take-backs now."

MaMá threw her hands in the air.

* * *

When they stepped out of the car in Chinatown, Ginny could feel the vibrations of the gongs and drums under her feet. "Listen!" she said to Stephanie. "They're almost ready for the parade."

"Let's get a good place," said Daddy, taking Ginny with one hand, Stephanie with the other.

"Look," said MaMá, pointing to the huge red banner carried by little kids and their parents.

Goosebumps popped up on Ginny's forearms. The parade was starting!

Bigger boys walked past, beating drums, and girls gently fanned themselves.

Ginny waved to the girls dancing with long ribbons attached to sticks. Some of them smiled back at her and gave their ribbons an extra flick.

Firecrackers popped everywhere.

The dragon was made of a long tube of cloth with five men underneath. The men hopped and turned, crisscrossed their feet and jumped to the music. The dragon had long fake eyelashes like MaMá's. The eyelashes fluttered as the huge eyes opened and shut.

"Oh, look, Stephanie. That's us. We're just like that powerful dragon!" Ginny shouted.

Stephanie tossed her hair. "It's a little silly, the way you see those guys' legs underneath. It looks more like a caterpillar than a dragon."

Yet she kept her eyes on the dragon—even standing on tiptoe to watch—until it was out of sight.

Dragon. When MaMá saw it prancing by, had she thought of Ginny's jade dragon? Maybe she would look for it on the shelf when she got home.

Ginny blushed. There went the magnificent dragon, thrashing and rising to the beat of the drums and gongs, the big moment of the New Year's parade, and her own dragon was at Stephanie's house, eating play food at a play table.

* * *

"The parking gods must be with us." Daddy drove into a spot as another car pulled out.

Suddenly, Ginny understood where Daddy was taking them. *Oh please, Daddy, not* this *restaurant!* she pleaded silently. Why couldn't they go to one of the fancy ones?

Daddy's special restaurant was on a dirty street covered with the wrappers of shot-off firecrackers, red ribbons, yellow-and-red banners, and noisemakers, all stepped on and smushed into the street. A staircase led down to the bottom floor of an old building. Ginny smelled pee as they went down the steps.

How could Daddy bring Stephanie to a place like this? She already didn't like Chinese food. Ginny gripped Stephanie's hand and held her breath.

Inside the restaurant, the plastic table covers

· 128 ·

and vinyl chairs didn't match. The yellow flowers on the wallpaper looked scratched. Pictures of the animals of the zodiac, the Buddha, and photographs of old buildings had been hung in no particular order.

A woman came forward, and looking at Ginny, said, "This is your girl?"

"Yes, this is Liao Xin Mei," said Daddy resting his hands on Ginny's shoulders.

The woman pinched Ginny's cheek. She talked really fast in Chinese, then broke into English: "You don't understand?"

Ginny shook her head no.

"How about you?" She pointed to Stephanie. "You don't understand either?"

"They are Americanized," MaMá said in English. "Stephanie is Xin Mei's *pang jau* from American school. But Xin Mei goes to Chinese School, and she is getting many praises for her calligraphy."

"What's *pang jau*?" Stephanie whispered in Ginny's ear.

"Friend," Ginny whispered back. She pulled her heart necklace from underneath her blouse so the woman could see that she and Stephanie were best friends.

The woman raised her eyebrows. She nodded at Stephanie, then took Ginny's chin in one hand and lifted her face.

The woman reached into her apron pocket. "Here." She handed each of them a box of four crayons. She pointed to a place mat, and then at Ginny. "You do calligraphy."

Everyone gathered around to watch as Ginny made each stroke with the clumsy crayon. She wrote her name, *Liao Xin Mei*.

Then MaMá wrote *Gong Xi Fa Cai,* and Ginny began to copy.

"She needs to make that stroke longer," said MaMá. "But it's okay."

Daddy leaned closer. "It looks good to me."

"Talented work," the woman said.

Stephanie was doodling her name, *Stephanie Lee Bronelle,* on her place mat and peeking at Ginny's calligraphy. Mrs. Vincent likes my art, she mumbled.

Daddy ordered Ginny's favorite *dim sum* dishes: tiny dumplings stuffed with chopped shrimp, rice crepes with shrimp and sweet soy sauce wrapped up inside, crab-claw puffs, and a pot of green tea.

MaMá ordered Ginny's favorite main dish: steamed fish with sliced green onions and a sweet brown sauce.

The woman came out with a huge plate. "Honored calligrapher and guests, here is our specialty. We made it very special for you, our best customers." She lowered the plate. On it was a roasted duck. The feet were still on it, spread wide on the plate. The head dangled sideways, the cooked eyes staring.

Stephanie gasped and looked away.

"What's wrong?" Ginny asked her.

Stephanie whispered into Ginny's ear, "It's horrible. You can see its face and eyes. And its feet. It reminds me of the ducks at the pond."

Ginny looked at the duck. A cooked duck had never reminded her of a living duck. Now it did. The poor neck was twisted. She said loudly, "Stephanie and I are too sad about the duck to eat it."

"Ah Mei, who taught you such bad manners?" MaMá said loudly. She pinched her eyebrows together and made her lips tight.

"I'm not eating that." Ginny crossed her arms. Stephanie must not think that she would eat a duck head.

"Then you are not eating anything," said MaMá.

Daddy said to the woman, *Dui bu qi.* I am so sorry."

"No problem. Kids today are different." The woman walked away. *"Xin shang.* Enjoy."

Then Daddy turned to Ginny. "We've heard enough out of you, Ah Mei." Daddy sounded mad. "We'll talk about this at the house."

MaMá picked up Ginny's plate.

Ginny put her head down on the table in the empty spot where her plate had been. As the dishes came to the table, Ginny could almost taste the delicious foods that Daddy and MaMá had ordered. She could hear them breaking the drumsticks off the duck.

When Ginny peeked at Stephanie's plate, she saw she was eating only rice with soy sauce. She was missing out on all the good stuff. Ginny wished that she hadn't invited Stephanie. Now Stephanie knew the worst secret—that Chinese people ate ducks with the heads still on.

The next morning, MaMá made rice porridge. When Ginny looked at it closely, there were chopped scallions on top and bits of meat. Could that meat be the duck meat left over from the restaurant?

Daddy had been reading the Chinese paper, but he folded it up as Ginny slid into her chair. "Virginia." He hardly ever used her American name when it was just them. "Your behavior at the restaurant was inappropriate. You are not to embarrass your mother and me again like that. Do you understand?"

"But Daddy, the head was still on the duck! And Stephanie saw it!"

"So what? Ducks have heads whether you see or not see." MaMá ladled rice porridge into Ginny's bowl. "Stop being so spoiled, Ah Mei. Listen to your *babá*."

Ginny gave up. "Yes, MaMá. Yes, Daddy. I'm sorry."

But as she ate the rice porridge, she shifted the bits of duck meat to the side and left them uneaten.

Chapter Eighteen

Ginny and MaMá were sitting on the couch in the family room watching MaMá's favorite show, *Wheel of Fortune.*

"Wheel! Of! Fortune!" MaMá and Ginny shouted together, in sync with the TV audience. The big wheel with the numbers on the edge spun around.

MaMá liked guessing the letters and watching the blocks blink up with a *Ding!* "The clue is noun." She scratched her chin.

"That's a person, place, or thing." Ginny said, remembering the chart in her classroom.

"I know, Ah Mei. I watch this show every night."

The contestant with the big glasses yelled, "I'll solve the puzzle. The answer is NAVY BRAT."

Cheers and clapping came from the TV.

"What is *brat*?" asked MaMá.

"A kid who is annoying, who whines a lot."

"I see. Like someone who is spoiled." MaMá mouthed the word, "brat."

At the end of a commercial for Kellogg's Frosted Flakes, Ginny said, "MaMá, tomorrow it's my turn for Show and Tell at school."

"Show? Tell? I do not understand, Ah Mei."

"I have to bring something interesting from home to show. Then I have to tell about it."

"Hmm." MaMá was watching an ad for panty hose. The TV camera moved close to show the lady's legs—shiny and smooth. "You could show and tell the postcards that BaBá brought back from Africa. Or you could show and tell the tiny Eiffel Tower he gave you from Paris. Those things are interesting."

"Maybe." Ginny tucked her feet up underneath her.

Suddenly, MaMá turned to look at Ginny, her eyes big. "I know what is perfect, Ah Mei."

Ginny swallowed hard. Was MaMá about to suggest the jade dragon? Of course. The dragon was the most important thing she owned. "What is perfect, MaMá?" she managed to say.

Vanna White, the lady who turned the big letters, was turning the letters again, standing a little to one side.

"You should tell and show what you did at Chinese School. Your calligraphy."

Ginny sighed with relief and straightened her legs.

She'd done the calligraphy on the piece of yellow paper. It had just been practice. She hadn't even used a brush. But she had to agree to share it or MaMá was sure to suggest the dragon. "The calligraphy is a good idea. That's what I'll take."

Ginny did her homework in the living room, on the table underneath the glass cabinet. That way, if MaMá came looking for the dragon, Ginny would know.

It was time to get the dragon back from Stephanie. Stephanie played with it every day and wouldn't want to let it go. If only Ginny had something she could give her in the dragon's place.

"It's Ginny's turn for Show and Tell today," Mrs. Vincent announced as the class gathered on the floor in a circle.

Ginny sat down next to Mrs. Vincent. She held her yellow paper in both hands, which were sticky with sweat. She hoped the class would like the calligraphy. She especially hoped Stephanie would like it.

"Go ahead, Ginny," said Mrs. Vincent. "The class is quiet now."

Ginny unfolded the yellow paper and held it up. She turned it to the right and to the left, so that everyone could see.

"Oooh," several kids said.

"Cool," said Ricky.

"Weird," Patty said.

"Wow," Elisa almost shouted.

Mrs. Vincent leaned closer. "How beautiful!"

Miss Yee had said the same thing: *This is beautiful.*

It must be true then. Her work was beautiful. Ginny sat like a tall mountain, her legs crossed.

She waited until everyone was quiet, just like Mrs. Vincent did. When she began to talk, her voice sounded calm and clear just like Mrs. Vincent's:

"I did this in my calligraphy class at Chinese School." She pointed to the Chinese characters that ran down the columns on the yellow paper. "Calligraphy is a special kind of writing."

Stephanie, like the others, was leaning forward to get a better look.

Jessica raised her hand. "What does it say?"

"This is my name." Ginny pointed to *Liao Xin Mei.* "And this says *mountain, tree,* and *river.* In Chinese, we use strokes to make letters. They're called characters. We write and read this way." She ran her fingertip from right to left.

Ricky raised his hand. "Your Chinese name looks so cool. Can you write my name in Chinese?"

"Me too?" asked Bryan.

And then a bunch of others asked, "Me too?" without even raising their hands.

Stephanie smiled at Ginny, as though saying a silent *Me too!*

Ginny began to call on people just the way Mrs. Vincent did, answering their questions.

"What does Chinese sound like?" Martin asked.

"Like this: *Zaoshang hao,*" said Ginny. "That means *good morning.*"

"Is it hard to learn to speak Chinese?"

"Very hard," Ginny answered.

"How long did it take you to learn to write like that?"

Ginny sat up even taller. "It might take you a long time. But it took me just one day because I'm Chinese."

At recess, a big bunch of kids came up to Ginny, begging her to write their names in Chinese.

"I can't write your names," she explained. "But I can write *my* name for you. I can also write *mountain, tree,* and *river.*"

So she wrote on their binders, on scraps of

paper, on the backs of school photos—whatever they handed her.

In the distance, Ginny saw Stephanie playing on the monkey bars. Later, she would write for Stephanie. She'd write Stephanie's words with a brush, on MaMá's rice paper. And then she would ask for the dragon back.

Chapter Nineteen

For homework, Ginny was writing a story using the week's vocabulary words: *The whale flipped over the boat. . . .*

She heard MaMá calling her from downstairs. Ginny lifted her head.

"Ah Mei, you must come down here right now," MaMá called again.

Ginny stood up slowly, then froze.

"Ah Mei, come now!"

Downstairs, instead of clinking her big chopsticks around and around in the wok, MaMá was rushing through the dining room, pulling the cushions off the chairs, yanking back the heavy curtains. The glass doors of the zodiac cabinet hung wide open.

Ginny stopped at the bottom of the staircase. It had finally happened.

"Ah Mei, have you seen the jade dragon? It is missing."

Ginny felt as if she was on an elevator going down so fast that her stomach arrived before the rest of her.

"Ah Mei, do not just stand there. Help me find it." MaMá was on her knees, searching under the dining-room table.

"Maybe you put it somewhere when you were cleaning."

The eleven animals in the case stared at her. Ginny turned away from them.

"Impossible. I have not dusted the animals." MaMá looked straight at Ginny. "The animals were not in their usual places."

Ginny peeled back a corner of the carpet, pretending to search. "Maybe Daddy took it to work for good luck."

"BaBá would not do that." MaMá brushed the loose strands of hair off her face. "Ah Mei, what could have happened to your dragon?"

"I don't know, MaMá." Ginny kicked the carpet back into place.

"Did you take it out to play with, Ah Mei?"

Ginny shook her head.

Suddenly, MaMá pointed at Ginny's hand and said, "What is that?"

Ginny looked down. Sunlight danced off Stephanie's ring and cast rainbows on the wall.

"Tell me. Now."

"Stephanie gave it to me."

"You are going to give that thing back to her.

You do not take anything from anybody. You are not a beggar."

Ginny looked down at the floor. Begging was shameful. She took a deep breath. "I didn't beg, MaMá. I traded with Stephanie."

MaMá got very still. "What? What did you trade?"

If she didn't tell the truth, MaMá would guess. "The dragon."

There was a long silence—even the jade animals seemed to be listening—and then MaMá shouted a bunch of words in Chinese.

Ginny covered her ears.

MaMá pulled Ginny's hands off her ears and, said in English, "Ah Mei, you should never have given your dragon away. Your *babá* had it carved just for you."

"It wasn't a forever trade, MaMá. Just for a little while."

"A little while. Forever. It does not matter."

MaMá slumped down onto the couch. "Ah Mei, that dragon was made from the jade that your *babá* gave you. Now look what you have done." She waved at the glass case. "The dragon always reminded me of you, Ah Mei. One day, I was going to give you the dragon and all the other animals. But now . . ."

Ginny wanted to go to MaMá and put her head on her lap. She wanted MaMá to smooth her hair. "MaMá? I . . ." She didn't know what to say.

"You are going to return that plastic thing and get your dragon back. You understand?"

"Yes, MaMá."

MaMá stood and marched upstairs.

Ginny hardly moved or breathed. She felt as if she was made out of stone, like the jade dragon.

She still felt like cold jade when Mrs. B. let her in at Stephanie's house. "Go on upstairs, honey." She patted Ginny's shoulder.

Stephanie lay on the canopy bed, reading. She glanced up when Ginny stood in the doorway. "Why are you crying, Ginny?"

"Stephanie-I-have-to-ask-for-the-dragon-back." Ginny spoke without taking a breath.

Stephanie closed the book.

"My mother found out the dragon is missing. I shouldn't have given it to you. My father had it made for me when I was a baby." Ginny stepped closer. "I shouldn't have traded with you."

Stephanie sat up, and the book fell to the floor. "But I gave *you* something precious. I let you use the ring my grandmother gave me."

"It's only plastic."

"It is not. It is real diamonds."

"My mom says—"

"I don't care what your mom says. Grandma Nancy said it was real diamonds. And she should know."

"Well, here it is, then."

Stephanie put the ring on her finger, then took it off and tossed it onto the dresser. "You might as well give back the necklace too."

Ginny reached around to the clasp of her heart necklace, her fingers shaking so much, she could hardly undo it. Then she laid the necklace on the bed beside Stephanie. "Now I need my dragon."

Stephanie went to her dresser and pulled open the sock drawer.

Ginny took a step closer, her hand ready.

Stephanie laid the green jade across Ginny's palm.

Then she opened another drawer. "Take this all back too. I don't want it." She tossed out the red *lai-see* envelope, notes they'd passed during class, and photos her mom had taken of them watching *The Smurfs*.

Ginny didn't bend down to pick up anything. She just stared at the pile. "Wow. I didn't know you kept all this stuff."

"We were friends."

"We're still friends. You're my best friend." Ginny stared at the poster above her bed. They'd made it one Saturday after *The Smurfs:* BEST FRIENDS 4-EVA. Would Stephanie rip that down?

"You've played with all my stuff all this time," said Stephanie. "I just ask for one little thing of yours—"

"It wasn't a little thing. It was really important."

Stephanie was quiet. After a moment, she said, "Was your mom really mad?"

Ginny nodded and sat down near Stephanie on the bed. She could smell the laundry-soap smell from the sheets.

"Did you tell her I wasn't going to keep it forever?"

Ginny nodded again.

Just then, she saw one of Stephanie's princess drawings lying on the bottom shelf of the nightstand. The princess had the usual long blond hair that swept behind her like a bride's train. But in the corner of the drawing were some funny markings. Ginny leaned closer to the drawing. The markings were Chinese characters. Sort of. Did they say *Liao Xin Mei*? Could it be? Had Stephanie been trying to do calligraphy?

Ginny picked up the drawing. "What's this?" she asked.

Stephanie sat up. "What's what?" When she saw the paper, she took it from Ginny's hand, wadded it up, and threw it in the wastebasket.

Chapter Twenty

When Ginny got home, she didn't hear MaMá in the kitchen cooking. She tiptoed in and took a peek. No MaMá. She looked down the stairway into the basement, and listened for MaMá doing laundry. Nothing.

Ginny opened the glass of the cabinet and slipped the dragon in. She didn't bother to move the other animals into their places. The dragon's torch of green fire touched the monkey's tail.

She went slowly up the stairs and saw that MaMá's bedroom door was shut.

Ginny walked quickly along the carpet to her own room.

She shut her door too. As she lay with her face in the pillow, seeing only blackness with tiny swirling stars, a terrible idea came to her—even worse than going to school in China. MaMá had shut her door. Did that mean that she was through with Ginny forever?

Was MaMá planning to give her away, just as Stephanie's parents had given *her* away?

Maybe she would be taken away before Daddy even got home. Maybe like Stephanie, she would never see her father again.

The sun went down, and Ginny got cold. She crawled under the blanket, making herself into a tight little ball.

Soon she smelled coconut curry cooking downstairs. MaMá must have called for a special delivery of Thai eggplants from the Eden Super-market. If she was through with Ginny, why was she cooking her favorite dish?

"Ah Mei, come for your dinner." Instead of calling up the stairs, MaMá spoke from outside Ginny's door.

Ginny pulled the blanket away from her face. She waited until she heard MaMá go downstairs again. Then she got up and went down to the kitchen.

She sat at the table, screwing up her face against the tears. Maybe a family from Chinese School would take her.

"Hmph," MaMá said as she set down a bowl of curry and a bowl of rice in front of Ginny. "The dragon is back with the others."

"I'm sorry, MaMá."

"Ah Mei, you cannot make people be your friend by giving them things. Especially things that do not belong to you." MaMá scratched her cheek with her red fingernail.

"I won't do it again." Ginny squeezed her napkin with both hands. "Please don't send me away, MaMá." And then she was crying into the coconut curry.

MaMá stepped closer. "Send you away? What foolish idea is that?"

Ginny looked up, squinting through the tears. "You mean you're keeping me?"

MaMá sat down beside her. "Of course, Ah Mei." She put her arm around Ginny's shoulder and pulled her close. "You are my little dragon."

Ginny leaned against MaMá, sniffing and wiping her face with her sleeve.

"Now eat," said MaMá.

Ginny scooped the round Thai eggplants over the rice. As she ate, her whole body became warm with the spices.

MaMá sat down across from Ginny, and they ate together without talking.

That night, Ginny heard Daddy come home late, the tires rolling across the driveway, the door of the garage squeaking open.

She put on her bathrobe and ran down to meet him as he came through the front door. She threw her arms around his waist. His coat was so cold!

"Whoa. Whoa." He lifted her so that her feet were hanging in the air. "Shouldn't little girls be in bed right now?"

"I just wanted to see you, Daddy." Ginny hugged his neck.

He hugged her back as though she'd done nothing wrong.

"All right. Let's get you to bed." Daddy carried Ginny up the stairs, snowflakes falling off his trench coat onto the carpeted steps.

"Now, go to bed, Ah Mei," Daddy said, laying

her down. "It's late. Whatever is going on in that little head of yours can wait for another day."

Daddy left the door open a bit, so that Ginny could see the light from the hallway. She could hear Daddy and MaMá talking downstairs. She got out of bed and pressed her ear to the floor. But even though she could hear better, she couldn't understand the secret Chinese words. Was MaMá telling Daddy about the dragon? Daddy might not hug her so tight once he knew.

In the morning, Ginny peeked into the kitchen to find Daddy and MaMá sitting together at the table, drinking tea.

MaMá was embroidering a pink chrysanthemum pillowcase, and Daddy was reading the Chinese newspaper.

When he saw Ginny, he folded the newspaper. "Hey there, how's my favorite daughter?" He held out one arm to her.

"I'm your only daughter," Ginny said, snuggling close.

"That's why you're my favorite." He kissed her.

Ginny smiled and kissed him back.

But then he said, "Your *mamá* told me about the dragon."

Ginny pulled back so that she could see his face. He wasn't smiling.

"I'm sorry, Daddy." Ginny began to cry.

Daddy drew her close again. "I can see you're sorry, Ah Mei."

Ginny wanted to stay like that forever, her face hidden in the warm red plaid of Daddy's bathrobe.

After a few minutes, MaMá said, "There is something else, Ah Mei. Mrs. B. called. She says Stephanie is very upset. You and Stephanie have a fight."

Stephanie. Ginny wanted to hide her face even more.

"Your fight is no big deal, Ah Mei. People fight all the time," MaMá said. "Just be friends again. Stephanie is a Chinese girl like you."

"But MaMá . . ." Ginny began.

"Yes. I know what I said. But I was not right. Stephanie is a little more Chinese than even you, Ah Mei," said MaMá. "You were born in *this* country."

Ginny listened to the washing machine down in the basement, swishing and burbling.

"Stephanie was born in China, and you were both born in the year of the dragon," MaMá said.

We go together. . . . Chang-chang changity-chang shoo-bop. That's the way it should be. . . . began to go through Ginny's head. The washer stopped, beeped three times, and started up again.

As MaMá stitched away at the petals of her flower, as Daddy went to get dressed for work, and as the washer spun with a loud clanking sound, Ginny traced over the characters in the Chinese newspaper with a pencil.

When the washer came to a final stop, Ginny laid down the pencil and said, "I'm going to need your help."

MaMá slid the needle into the cloth, then looked up. "What help?"

Ginny spread out a piece of newspaper on the kitchen table. She went to the cabinet and took out rice paper and MaMá's brush and ink.

First she wrote the note in English. "Now, MaMá, please write this in characters, so I can copy it."

MaMá wrote quickly on a plain piece of paper. "You think this will work, Ah Mei?" she asked. "You and Stephanie will be friends again, right?"

"I hope so, MaMá."

MaMá squinted at her Chinese-English dictionary and read the characters out loud, looking for the best way to say things.

When Ginny began to copy, she wrote slowly, studying the parts of each character, the angle of the lines, the shapes the character made inside and outside itself.

Sometimes MaMá's hand covered Ginny's hand, her skin warm against Ginny's. "Push this stroke down a little," she said, guiding her. "Hold the bamboo rod at this angle."

"Now good," she said at last.

Ginny lifted the wet rice paper and blew it dry.

Chapter Twenty-one

The next day, Ginny waited for Stephanie at the top of the school steps, her heart beating like a drum in the Chinese New Year's parade.

Stephanie didn't look up as she climbed. When she got to the top, Ginny handed her the rectangular package.

Stephanie tore away the brown wrapping paper and tilted her head to the side. "What is it?"

Ginny pointed to a column of characters. "This is your name banner. My mom and I painted it, and then we framed it for you." The lines of Chinese letters looked very black in the early morning light.

"It's in Chinese?"

"Yup. But it's not your American name. It's your new Chinese name, *Mai Pang Jau.*"

"That's long. What does it mean?"

"*Beautiful Friend.* My mom suggested it."

"It's pretty."

"And I have this for you." Ginny handed Stephanie a scroll.

Stephanie unrolled the paper. "What does it say?"

Ginny's heart drummed harder. "It's an invitation for you to come to Chinese School next Saturday." She swallowed. "You're so good at drawing, calligraphy will be easy for you too. We can spend Saturdays together again."

Stephanie sat down on the step, still holding the paper.

Ginny sat down beside her. After a moment, she moved a little closer.

A breeze came up, pushing leaves together into a pile.

Stephanie unrolled the invitation again and pointed to the black characters. "At Chinese School, could I really learn to write like this?"

"You could."

"You know I don't like Chinese stuff."

Ginny thought of the characters on Stephanie's drawing. "Just the calligraphy, Stephanie. Just try it."

"Maybe." Stephanie sighed.

The breeze tossed the pile of leaves along the sidewalk.

"*Mai Pang Jau,*" Stephanie said softly to herself. Then she looked at Ginny. "What was *your* name again?"

"Xin Mei."

"Xin Mei," Stephanie repeated. She reached

into her pocket and took out the two half-heart necklaces. She handed one to Ginny.

Ginny closed her hand around the chain, still warm from Stephanie's pocket. She scooted even closer, so that their shoulders touched. "Mai Pang Jau," she began, then coughed and went on, "will you be my beautiful friend?"

Stephanie reached over and opened Ginny's fist. She picked up the half heart and fit it to hers. "We make one whole heart," she said, and smiled.

GLOSSARY

义燒 ***chau-su:*** red pork

蛋撻 ***dan-tat:*** custard tart

點心 ***dim sum:*** (Cantonese) Chinese appetizers

對不起 ***dui bu qi:*** I'm sorry

父親 ***fu qin:*** Father/BaBá

恭喜發財 ***Gong Xi Fa Cai!:*** (Cantonese) Happy Chinese New Year!

紅包 ***lai-see:*** (Cantonese) red envelope containing gift money

廖心美 ***Liao Xin Mei***

美朋友 ***mai pang jau:*** (Cantonese) beautiful friend

母親 ***mu qin:*** Mother/MaMá

朋友 ***pang jau:*** (Cantonese) friend

心美 ***Xin Mei:*** Beautiful Heart

欣賞 ***xin shang:*** enjoy

玉龍 ***yu lung:*** jade dragon

早上好 ***zaoshang hao:*** (Cantonese) good morning

再見 ***zai jian:*** good-bye

字譜 ***zha pu:*** glossary